THE BLOOMSBURY GROUP

EX LIBRIS

THE BLOOMSBURY GROUP

A NOTE ON THE AUTHOR

ADA LEVERSON (*née* Beddington) was born in London on 10 October 1862. Her father was a wool merchant resident in Hyde Park and her mother was an outstanding pianist. Leverson was educated at home and became well read in English, French and German literature and the classics. At the age of nineteen she married, against her parents' wish, Ernest Leverson, twelve years her senior. She gave birth to a son, who survived only twenty-one weeks, and a daughter.

From the age of thirty Leverson published stories and sketches in *Punch* and other periodicals, including *The Yellow Book* (the former being accompanied by a portrait-drawing of her by Walter Sickert). She also became well-known in London society for her witty, outrageous remarks. Her friends included Aubrey Beardsley, Max Beerbohm, Mrs Patrick Campbell and most notably, Oscar Wilde, who christened her his 'Sphinx'. During Wilde's infamous trial in 1895 Leverson took Wilde into her home and when she was the first person to greet him upon his release from prison two years later he exclaimed, 'Sphinx, how marvellous of you to know exactly the right hat to wear at seven o'clock in the morning to meet a friend who has been away.'

After separating from her husband in 1902, and with many of her dear friends dead, Leverson published six classic comedies of manners: *The Twelfth Hour* (1907), *Love's Shadow* (1908), *The Limit* (1911), *Tenterhooks* (1912), *Birds of Paradise* (1914) and *Love at Second Sight* (1916). *Love's Shadow*, *Tenterhooks* and *Love at Second Sight* were first published together as the trilogy *The Little Ottleys* by MacGibbon & Kee in 1962. Her last published book was *Letters to the Sphinx from Oscar Wilde, with Reminiscences of the Author* (1930). In her later years her friends included Harold Acton, William Walton and the Sitwells.

Ada Leverson died at her home in Mayfair on 30 August 1933.

First published in 1908
This paperback edition published 2009 by Bloomsbury Publishing Plc

Bloomsbury Publishing Plc, 36 Soho Square, London W1D 3QY

Ex libris illustration © 2009 by Penelope Beech

A CIP catalogue record for this book is available from
the British Library

ISBN 978 1 4088 0382 0

10 9 8 7 6 5 4 3 2

Printed in Great Britain by Clays Ltd, St Ives plc

Typeset by Macmillan Publishing Solutions
www.macmillansolutions.com

All papers used by Bloomsbury Publishing are natural, recyclable
products made from wood grown in well-managed forests. The
manufacturing processes conform to the environmental regulations
of the country of origin

www.bloomsbury.com/thebloomsburygroup

Love's Shadow

Ada Leverson

B L O O M S B U R Y

LONDON · BERLIN · NEW YORK

Love's Shadow

Love like a shadow flies
    When substance love pursues;
Pursuing that that flies,
    And flying what pursues.

SHAKESPEARE

Hyacinth

'THERE'S only one thing I must really implore you, Edith,' said Bruce anxiously. '*Don't* make me late at the office!'

'Certainly not, Bruce,' answered Edith sedately. She was seated opposite her husband at breakfast in a very new, very small, very white flat in Knightsbridge - exactly like thousands of other new, small, white flats. She was young and pretty, but not obvious. One might suppose that she was more subtle than was shown by her usual expression, which was merely cheerful and intelligent.

'Now I have to write that letter before I go,' Bruce exclaimed, starting up and looking at her reproachfully. 'Why didn't I write it last night?'

Edith hadn't the slightest idea, as she had heard nothing of the letter before, but, in the course of three years, she had learnt that it saved time to accept trifling injustices. So she looked guilty and a little remorseful. He magnanimously forgave her, and began to write the letter at a neat white writing-table.

'How many g's are there in "Raggett"?' he asked suspiciously.

She didn't answer, apparently overtaken by a sudden fit of absence of mind.

'Only one, of course. How absurd you are!' said her husband, laughing, as he finished the letter and came back to the table.

She poured out more coffee.

'It's a curious thing,' he went on in a tone of impartial regret, 'that, with all the fuss about modern culture and higher education nowadays, girls are not even taught to spell!'

'Yes, isn't it? But even if I had been taught, it might not have been much use. I might just not have been taught to spell "Raggett". It's a name, isn't it?'

'It's a very well-known name,' said Bruce.

'I daresay it is, but I don't know it. Would you like to see the boy before you go?'

'What a question! I always like to see the boy. But you know perfectly well I haven't time this morning.'

'Very well, dear. You can see him this afternoon.'

'Why do you say that? You know I'm going golfing with Goldthorpe! It really is hard, Edith, when a man has to work so much that he has scarcely any time for his wife and child.'

She looked sympathetic.

'What are you doing today?' he asked.

'Hyacinth's coming to fetch me for a drive in the motor.'

His face brightened. He said kindly, 'I *am* so glad, darling, that you have such a delightful friend – when I can't be with you. I admire Hyacinth very much, in every way. She seems devoted to you, too, which is really very nice of her. What I mean to say is, that in her position she might know anybody. You see my point?'

'Quite.'

'How did you meet her originally?'

'We were school-friends.'

'She's such a lovely creature; I wonder she doesn't marry.'

'Yes, but she has to find someone else whom *she* thinks a lovely creature, too.'

'Edith, dear.'

'Yes, Bruce.'

'I wish you wouldn't snap me up like that. Oh, I know you don't mean it, but it's growing on you, rather.'

She tried to look serious, and said gently, 'Is it, really? I am sorry.'

'You don't mind me telling you of it, do you?'

'Not at all. I'm afraid you will be late, Bruce.'

He started up and hurried away, reminding Edith that dinner was to be at eight. They parted with affectionate smiles.

When he had gone down in the lift, Edith took an inextensive walk through the entire flat, going into each room, and looking at herself in every looking-glass. She appeared to like herself best in the dining-room mirror, for she returned, stared into it rather gravely for some little time, and then said to herself: 'Yes, I'm beginning to look bored.'

Then she rang the bell, and the nurse brought in a pretty little boy of nearly two, fluffily dressed in white, who was excited at the prospect of his great morning treat – going down in the lift. Speaking of him with some formality as Master Archie, she asked the nurse a few questions, which she mistakenly supposed gave that personage the impression that she knew all that there was to be known about children. When she was alone with him for a minute she rushed at him impulsively, saying, privately, 'Heavenly pet! Divine angel! Duck!' in return for which he pulled her hair down and scratched her face with a small empty Noah's Ark that he was taking out with him for purposes of his own.

When he had gone she did her hair up again in a different way - parted in the middle. It was very pretty, wavy, fair hair, and she had small, regular features, so the new way suited her very well. Then she said again -

'Yes, if it were not for Hyacinth I should soon look bored to death!'

Hyacinth Verney was the romance of Edith's life. She also provided a good deal of romance in the lives of several other people. Her position was unusual, and her personality fascinating. She had no parents, was an heiress, and lived alone with a companion in a quaint little house just out of Berkeley Square, with a large studio that was never used for painting. She had such an extraordinary natural gift for making people of both sexes fond of her, that it would have been difficult to say which, of all the persons who loved her, showed the most intense devotion in the most immoderate way. Probably her cousin and guardian, Sir Charles Cannon, and her companion, Anne Yeo, spent more thought and time in her service than did anybody else. Edith's imagination had been fired in their school-days by her friend's beauty and cleverness, and by the fact that she had a guardian, like a book. Then Hyacinth had come out and gone in for music, for painting, and for various other arts and pursuits of an absorbing character. She had hardly any acquaintances except her relations, but possessed an enormously large number of extremely intimate friends - a characteristic that had remained to her from her childhood.

Hyacinth's ideal of society was to have no padding, so that most of the members of her circle were types. Still, as she had a perfect passion for entertaining, there remained, of course, a residue; distant elderly connections with well-sounding names (as ballast), and a few vague hangers-on; several rather dull celebrities, some merely pretty and well-dressed women, and a steadily increasing number of good-looking young men. Hyacinth was fond of decoration.

As she frankly admitted, she had rather fallen back on Edith, finding her, after many experiments, the most agreeable of friends, chiefly because in their intercourses everything was always taken for granted. Like sisters, they understood one another without explanation - *à demi-mot.*

While Edith waited impatiently in the hall of the flat, Anne Yeo, her unacknowledged rival in Hyacinth's affections, was doing needlework in the window-seat of the studio, and watching Hyacinth, who, dressed to go out, was walking up and down the room. With a rather wooden face, high cheek-bones, a tall, thin figure, and no expression, Anne might have been any age; but she was not. She made every effort to look quite forty so as to appear more suitable as a chap-erone, but was in reality barely thirty. She was thinking, as she often thought, that Hyacinth looked too romantic for everyday life. When they had travelled together, this fact had been rather a nuisance.

'Why, when you call at the Stores to order groceries, must you look as if you were going to elope?' she asked dryly. 'In an ordinary motorveil you have the air of hastening to some mysterious appointment.'

'But I'm only going to fetch Edith Ottley for a drive,' said Hyacinth. 'How bored she must get with her little Foreign Office clerk! The way he takes his authority as a husband seriously is pathetic. He hasn't the faintest idea the girl is cleverer than he is.'

'You'd far better leave her alone, and not point it out,' said Anne. 'You're always bothering about these little Ottleys now. But you've been very restless lately. Whenever you try to do people good, and especially when you motor so much and so fast, I recognise the symptoms. It's coming on again, and you're trying to get away from it.'

'Don't say that. I'm never going to care about anyone again,' said Hyacinth.

'You don't know it, but when you're not in love you're not yourself,' Anne continued. 'It's all you live for.'

'Oh, Anne!'

'It's quite true. It's nearly three months since you – had an attack. Blair was the last. Now you're beginning to take the same sort of interest in Cecil Reeve.'

'How mistaken you are, Anne! I don't take at all the same interest in him. It's a totally different thing. I don't really even like him.'

'You wouldn't go out today if you were expecting him.'

'Yes, but I'm not . . . and he doesn't care two straws about me. Once he said he never worshipped in a crowded temple!'

'It's a curious coincidence that ever since then you've been out to everyone else,' said Anne.

'I don't really like him – so very much. When he *does* smile, of course it's rather nice. Why does he hate me?'

'I can't think,' said Anne.

'He doesn't hate me! How can you say so?' cried Hyacinth. 'Doesn't he?'

'Perhaps it's because he thinks I look Spanish. He may disapprove of looking Spanish,' suggested Hyacinth.

'Very likely.'

Hyacinth laughed, kissed her, and went out. Anne followed her graceful figure with disapproving, admiring eyes.

The anxieties of Sir Charles

LIKE all really uncommon beauties, Hyacinth could only be adequately described by the most hackneyed phrases. Her eyes were authentically sapphire-coloured; brilliant, frank eyes, with a subtle mischief in them, softened by the most conciliating long eyelashes. Then, her mouth was really shaped like a Cupid's bow, and her teeth *were* dazzling; also she had a wealth of dense, soft, brown hair and a tall, sylph-like, slimly-rounded figure. Her features were delicately regular, and her hands and feet perfection. Her complexion was extremely fair, so she was not a brunette; some remote Spanish ancestor on her mother's side was, however, occasionally mentioned as an apology for a type and a supple grace sometimes complained of by people with white eye-lashes as rather un-English. So many artistic young men had told her she was like La Gioconda, that when she first saw the original in the Louvre she was so disappointed that she thought she would never smile again.

About ten minutes after the pretty creature had gone out, Anne, who had kept her eyes steadily on the clock, looked out of the window, from which she could see a small brougham driving up. She called out into the hall –

'If that's Sir Charles Cannon, tell him Miss Verney is out, but I have a message for him.'

A minute later there entered a thin and distinguished-looking, grey-haired man of about forty-five, wearing a smile of such excessive cordiality that one felt it could only have been brought to his well-bred lips by acute disappointment. Anne did not take the smile literally, but began to explain away the blow.

'I'm so sorry,' she said apologetically. 'I'm afraid it's partly my fault. When she suddenly decided to go out with that little Mrs Ottley, she told me vaguely to telephone to you. But how on earth could I know where you were?'

'How indeed? It doesn't matter in the least, my dear Miss Yeo. I mean, it's most unfortunate, as I've just a little free time. Lady Cannon's gone to a matinée at the St James's. We had tickets for the first night, but of course she wouldn't use them then. She preferred to go alone in the afternoon, because she detests the theatre, anyhow, and afternoon performances give her a headache. And if she does a thing that's disagreeable to her, she likes to do it in the most painful possible way. She has a beautiful nature.'

Anne smiled, and passed him a little gold box.

'Have a cigarette?' she suggested.

'Thanks – I'm not really in a bad temper. But why this relapse of devotion to little Mrs Ottley? And why are you and I suddenly treated with marked neglect?'

'Mrs Ottley,' said Anne, 'is one of those young women, rather bored with their husbands, who are the worst possible companions for Hyacinth. They put her off marrying.'

'Bored, is she? She didn't strike me so. A pleasant, bright girl. I suppose she amuses Hyacinth?'

'Yes; of course, she's not a dull old maid over forty, like me,' said Anne.

'No-one would believe that description of you,' said Sir Charles, with a bow that was courtly but absent. As a matter of fact, he did believe it, but it wasn't true.

'If dear little Mrs Ottley,' he continued, 'married in too great a hurry, far be it from me to reproach her. I married in a hurry myself – when Hyacinth was ten.'

'And when she was eighteen you were very sorry,' said Anne in her colourless voice.

'Don't let us go into that, Miss Yeo. Of course, Hyacinth is a beautiful – responsibility. People seem to think she ought to have gone on living with us when she left school. But how was it possible? Hyacinth said she intended to live for her art, and Lady Cannon couldn't stand the scent of oils.' He glanced round the large panelled-oak room in which not a picture was to be seen. The only indication of its having ever been meant for a studio was the north light, carefully obstructed (on the grounds of unbecomingness) by gently-tinted draperies of some fabric suggesting Liberty's. 'Life wasn't worth living, trying to keep the peace!'

'But you must have missed her?'

'Still, I prefer coming to see her here. And knowing she has you with her is, after all, everything.'

He looked a question.

'Yes, she has. I mean, she seems rather – absorbed again lately,' said Anne.

'Who is it?' he asked. 'I always feel so indiscreet and treacherous talking over her private affairs like this with you, though she tells me everything herself. I'm not sure it's the act of a simple, loyal, Christian English gentleman; in fact, I'm pretty certain it's not. I suppose that's why I enjoy it so much.'

'I daresay,' said Anne; 'but she wouldn't mind it.'

'What has been happening?'

'Nothing interesting. Hazel Kerr came here the other day and brought with him a poem in bronze lacquer, as he called it. He read it aloud – the whole of it.'

'Good heavens! Poetry! Do people still do that sort of thing? I thought it had gone out years ago – when I was a young man.'

'Of course, so it has. But Hazel Kerr is out of date. Hyacinth says he's almost a classic.'

'His verses?'

'Oh no! His method. She says he's an interesting survival – he's walked straight out of another age – the nineties, you know. There were poets in those days.'

'Method! He was much too young then to have a style at all, surely!'

'That *was* the style. It was the right thing to be very young in the nineties. It isn't now.'

'It's not so easy now, for some of us,' murmured Sir Charles.

'But Hazel keeps it up,' Anne answered.

Sir Charles laughed irritably. 'He keeps it up, does he? But he sits people out openly, that shows he's not really dangerous. One doesn't worry about Hazel. It's that young man who arrives when everybody's going, or goes before anyone else arrives, that's what I'm a little anxious about.'

'If you mean Cecil Reeve, Hyacinth says he doesn't like her.'

'I'm sorry to hear that. If anything will interest her, that will. Yet I don't know why I should mind. At any rate, he certainly isn't trying to marry her for interested reasons, as he's very well off – or perhaps for any reasons. I'm told he's clever, too.'

CHAPTER TWO

'His appearance is not against him either,' said Anne dryly; 'so what's the matter with him?'

'I don't know exactly. I think he's capable of playing with her.'

'Perhaps he doesn't really appreciate her,' suggested Anne.

'Oh, yes, he does. He's a connoisseur – confound him! He appreciates her all right. But it's all for himself – not for her. By the way, I've heard his name mentioned with another woman's name. But I happen to know there's nothing in it.'

'Would you really like her to marry soon?' Anne asked.

'In her position it would be better, I suppose,' said her guardian, with obvious distaste to the idea.

'Has there ever been anyone that you thoroughly approved of?' asked Anne.

He shook his head.

'I rather doubt if there ever will be,' Anne said.

'She's so clever, so impulsive! She lives so much on her emotions. If she were disappointed – in that way – it would mean so much to her,' Sir Charles said.

'She does change rather often,' said Anne.

'Of course, she's never really known her own mind.' He took a letter out of his pocket. 'I came partly to show her a letter from Ella – my girl at school in Paris, you know. Hyacinth is so kind to her. She writes to me very confidentially. I hope she's being properly brought up!'

'Let me read it.'

She read –

DARLING PAPA,

I'm having heavenly fun at school. Last night there was a ball for Madame's birthday. A proper grown-up ball, and we all danced. The men weren't bad. I had a lovely Easter egg, a chocolate egg, and inside that another egg with chocolate in it, and inside that another egg with a dear little turquoise charm in it. One man said I was a blonde anglaise, and had a keepsake face; and another has taken the Prix de Rome, and is going to be a schoolmaster. There were no real ices. Come over and see me soon. It's such a long time to the holidays. Love to mother.

Your loving,
ELLA

'A curious letter – for her age,' said Ella's father, replacing it. 'I wish she were here. It seems a pity Lady Cannon can't stand the noise of practising – and so on. Well, perhaps it's for the best.' He got up. 'Miss Yeo, I must go and fetch Lady Cannon now, but I'll come back at half-past six for a few minutes – on my way to the club.'

'She's sure to be here then,' replied Anne consolingly; 'and do persuade her not to waste all her time being kind to Edith Ottley. It can't do any good. She'd better leave them alone.'

'Really, it's a very innocent amusement. I think you're overanxious.'

'It's only that I'm afraid she might get mixed up in – well, some domestic row.'

'Surely it can't be as bad as that! Why – is Mr Ottley in love with her?' he asked, smiling.

'Very much indeed,' said Anne.

'Oh, really, Miss Yeo! – and does Mrs Ottley know it?'

'No, nor Hyacinth either. He doesn't know it himself.'

'Then if nobody knows it, it can't matter very much,' said Sir Charles, feeling vaguely uncomfortable all the same. Before he went he took up a portrait of Hyacinth in an Empire dress with laurel leaves in her hair. It was a beautiful portrait. Anne thought that from the way he looked at it, anyone could have guessed Lady Cannon had tight lips and wore a royal fringe.... They parted with great friendliness.

Anne's wooden, inexpressive countenance was a great comfort to Sir Charles, in some moods. Though she was clever enough, she did not have that superfluity of sympathy and responsiveness that makes one go away regretting one has said so much, and disliking the other person for one's expansion. One never felt that she had understood too accurately, nor that one had given oneself away, nor been indiscreetly curious.... It was like talking to a chair. What a good sort Anne was!

Anne Yeo

'WOULD you like me to play to you a little?' Anne asked, when Hyacinth had returned and was sitting in the carved-oak chimney-corner, looking thoughtful and picturesque.

'Oh no, please don't! Besides, I know you can't.'

'No, thank goodness!' exclaimed Anne. 'I know I'm useful and practical, and I don't mind that; but anyhow, I'm not cheerful, musical, and a perfect lady, in exchange for a comfortable home, am I?'

'No, indeed,' said Hyacinth fervently.

'No-one can speak of me as "that pleasant, cultivated creature who lives with Miss Verney", can they?'

'Not, at any rate, if they have any regard for truth,' said Hyacinth.

'I wish you wouldn't make me laugh. Why should I have a sense of humour? I sometimes think that all your friends imagine it's part of my duty to shriek with laughter at their wretched jokes. It wasn't in the contract. If I were pretty, my ambition would have been to be an adventuress; but an adventuress with no adventures would be a little flat. I might have the worst intentions, but I should never have the chance of carrying them out. So I try to be as much as possible like Thackeray's shabby companion in a dyed silk.'

'Is that why you wear a sackcloth blouse trimmed with ashes?' said Hyacinth, with curiosity.

'No, that's merely stinginess. It's my nature to be morbidly economical, though I know I needn't be. If I hadn't had £500 a year left me, I should never have been able to come and live here, and drop all my horrid relations. I enjoy appearing dependent and being a spectator, and I've absolutely given up all interest in my own affairs. In fact, I haven't got any. And I take the keenest interest in other people's – romances. Principally, of course, in yours.'

'I'm sure I don't want you to be so vicarious as all that – thanks awfully,' said Hyacinth. 'At any rate, don't dress like a skeleton at the feast tomorrow, if you don't mind. I've asked the little Ottleys to dinner – and I want Charles to come.'

'Oh, of course, if you expect Cecil Reeve! – I suppose you do, as you haven't mentioned it – I'll put on my real clothes to do you credit.' She looked out of the window. 'Here's poor old Charles again. How he *does* dislike Lady Cannon!'

'What a shame, Anne! He's angelic to her.'

'That's what I meant,' said Anne, going out quickly.

'Charles, how nice of you to call and return your own visit the same day! It's like Royalty, isn't it? It reminds me of the young man who was asked to call again, and came back in half an hour,' said Hyacinth.

'I didn't quite see my way to waiting till Monday,' he answered. 'We're going away the end of the week. Janet says she needs a change.'

'It would be more of a change if you remained in town alone; at least, without Aunty.'

From the age of ten Hyacinth had resented having to call Lady Cannon by this endearing name. How a perfect stranger, by marrying her cousin, could become her aunt, was a mystery that she refused even to try to solve. It was well meant, no doubt; it was supposed to make her feel more at home – less of an orphan. But though she was obedient on this point, nothing would ever induce her to call her cousin by anything but his Christian name, with no quali-fication. Instinctively she felt that to call them 'Charles and Aunty', while annoying the intruder, kept her guardian in his proper place. What that was she did not specify.

'Well, can't you stay in London and come here, and be confided in and consulted? You know you like that better than boring yourself to death at Redlands.'

'Never mind that. How did you enjoy your drive?'

'Immensely, and I've asked both the little Ottleys to come to dinner tomorrow – one of those impulsive, uncon-sidered invitations that one regrets the second after. I must make up a little party. Will you come?'

'Perhaps, if I arranged to follow Janet to Redlands the next day, I might. Who did you say was the other man?'

'I expect Cecil Reeve,' she said. 'Don't put on that air of marble archness, Charles. It doesn't suit you at all. Tell me something about him.'

'I can't stand him. That's all I know about him,' said Sir Charles.

'Oh, is that all? That's just jealousy, Charles.'

'Absurd! How can a married man, in your father's place, a hundred years older than you, be jealous?'

'It is wonderful, isn't it?' she said. 'But you must know something about him. You know everyone.'

'He's Lord Selsey's nephew – and his heir – if Selsey doesn't marry again. He's only a young man about town – the sort of good-looking ass that your sex admires.'

'Charles, what a brute you are! He's very clever.'

'My dear child, yes – as a matter of fact, I believe he is. Isn't he ever going to *do* something?'

'I don't know,' she said. 'I wish he would. Oh, *why* don't you like him?'

'What can it matter about me?' he answered. 'Why are you never satisfied unless I'm in love with the same people that you are?'

'Charles!' she exclaimed, standing up. 'Don't you understand that not a word, not a look has passed to suggest such a thing? I never met anyone so – '

'So cautious?'

'No, so listless, and so respectful; and yet so amusing. . . . But I'm pretty certain that he hates me. I wish I knew why.'

'And you hate him just as much, of course?'

'No, sometimes I don't. And then I want you to agree with me. No-one sympathises really so well as you, Charles.'

'Not even Miss Yeo?'

'No, I get on so well with Anne because she doesn't. She's always interested, but I prefer her never to agree with me, as she lives here. It would be enervating to have someone always there and perpetually sympathetic. Anne is a tonic.'

'You need a little opposition to keep you up,' said Sir Charles.

'Didn't I once hear something about his being devoted to someone? Wasn't there a report that he was going to be married to a Mrs Raymond?'

'I believe it was once contradicted in the *Morning Post* that he was engaged to her,' said Sir Charles. 'But I'm sure there's no truth in it. I know her.'

'No truth in the report? Or the contradiction?'

'In either. In anything.'

'So you know her. What's she like?' Hyacinth asked anxiously.

'Oh, a dear, charming creature – you'd like her; but not pretty, nor young. About my age,' he said.

'Oh, I see! *That's* all right, then!' She clapped her hands.

'Well, I must go. I'll arrange to turn up to dinner tomorrow.' He took his hat, looking rather depressed.

'And try to make him like me!' she commanded, as Sir Charles took leave.

The sound sense of Lady Cannon

LADY CANNON had never been seen after half-past seven except in evening dress, generally a velvet dress of some dark crimson or bottle-green, so tightly-fitting as to give her an appearance of being rather upholstered than clothed. Her cloaks were always like well-hung curtains, her trains like heavy carpets; one might fancy that she got her gowns from Gillows. Her pearl dog-collar, her diamond ear-rings, her dark red fringe and the other details of her toilette were put on with the same precision when she dined alone with Sir Charles as if she were going to a ceremonious reception. She was a very tall, fine-looking woman. In Paris, where she sometimes went to see Ella at school, she attracted much public attention as *une femme superbe.* Frenchmen were heard to remark to one another that her husband *ne devrait pas s'embêter* (which, as a matter of fact, was precisely what he did – to extinction); and even in the streets when she walked out the gamins used to exclaim, '*Voilà l'Arc de Triomphe qui se promène!*' – to her intense fury and gratification. She was still handsome, with hard, wide-open blue eyes, and straight features. She always held her head as if she were being photographed in a tiara *en profil perdu*. It was in this attitude that she had often been photographed and was now most usually seen; and it seemed so characteristic that even her husband, if he accidentally caught a glimpse of her full-face, hastily altered his position to one whence he could behold her at right angles.

As she grew older, the profile in the photographs had become more and more *perdu*; the last one showed chiefly the back of her head, besides a basket of flowers, and a double staircase, leading (one hoped) at least to one of the upper rooms in Buckingham Palace.

Lady Cannon had a very exalted opinion of her own charms, virtues, brilliant gifts, and, above all, of her sound sense. Fortunately for her, she had married a man of extraordinary amiability, who had always taken every possible precaution to prevent her discovering that in this opinion she was practically alone in the world.

Having become engaged to her through a slight misunderstanding in a country house, Sir Charles had not had the courage to explain away the mistake. He decided to make the best of it, and did so the more easily as it was one of those so-called suitable matches that the friends and acquaintances of both parties approve of and desire far more than the parties concerned. A sensible woman was surely required at Redlands and in the London house, especially as Sir Charles had been left guardian and trustee to a pretty little heiress.

It had taken him a very short time to find out that the reputation for sound sense was, like most traditions, founded on a myth, and that if his wife's vanity was only equalled by her egotism, her most remarkable characteristic was her excessive silliness. But she loved him, and he kept his discovery to himself.

CHAPTER FOUR

'Twenty-five minutes to eight!' she exclaimed, holding out a little jewelled watch, as Sir Charles came in after his visit to Hyacinth. 'And we have a new cook, and I specially, *most* specially told her to have dinner ready punctually at half-past seven! This world is indeed a place of trial!'

Sir Charles's natural air of command seemed to disappear in the presence of Lady Cannon. He murmured a graceful apology, saying he would not dress. Nothing annoyed, even shocked her more than to see her husband dining opposite her in a frock-coat. However, of two evils she chose the less. They went in to dinner.

'I haven't had the opportunity yet of telling you my opinion of the play this afternoon,' she said. 'I found it interesting, and I wonder I hadn't seen it before.'

'You sent back our stalls for the first night,' remarked Sir Charles.

'Certainly I did. I dislike seeing a play until I have seen in the papers whether it is a success or not.'

'Those newspaper fellows aren't always right,' said Sir Charles.

'Perhaps not, but at least they can tell you whether the thing is a success. *I* should be very sorry to be seen at a failure. Very sorry indeed.'

She paused, and then went on –

'*James Wade's Trouble* has been performed three hundred times, so it must be clever. In my opinion, it must have done an immense amount of harm – good, I mean. A play like that, so full of noble sentiments and high principles, is – to me – as good as a sermon!'

'Oh, is it? I'm sorry I couldn't go,' said Sir Charles, feeling very glad.

'I suppose it was the club, as usual, that made you late. Do you know, I have a great objection to clubs.'

He nodded sympathetically.

'That is to say, I thoroughly approve of your belonging to several. I'm quite aware that in your position it's the right thing to do, but I can't understand why you should ever go to them, having two houses of your own. And that reminds me, we are going down to Redlands tomorrow, are we not? I've had a little' (she lowered her voice) 'lumbago; a mere passing touch, that's all – and the change will cure me. I think you neglect Redlands, Charles. You seem to me to regard your responsibilities as a landowner with indifference bordering on aversion. You never seem amused down there – unless we have friends.'

'We'll go tomorrow if you like,' said he.

'That's satisfactory.'

'I can easily put off the Duke,' he said thoughtfully, as he poured out more wine.

She sprang up like a startled hare.

'Put off the . . . what are you talking about?'

'Oh, nothing. The Duke of St Leonard's is giving a dinner at the club tomorrow, and I was going. But I can arrange to get out of it.'

'Charles! I never heard of anything so absurd! You must certainly go to the dinner. How like you! How casual of you! For a mere trifle to offend the man who might be of the greatest use to you – politically.'

'Politically! What do you mean? And it isn't a trifle when you've set your mind on going away tomorrow. I know you hate to change your plans, my dear.'

'Certainly I do, but I shall not change my plans. I shall go down tomorrow, and you can join me on Friday.'

'Oh, I don't think I'll do that,' said Sir Charles, rather half-heartedly. 'Why should you take the journey alone?'

CHAPTER FOUR

'But I shall not be alone. I shall have Danvers with me. You need have no anxiety. I beg of you, I *insist*, that you stay, and go to this dinner.'

'Well, of course, if you make a point of it – '

She smiled, well pleased at having got her own way, as she supposed.

'That's right, Charles. Then you'll come down on Friday.'

'By the early train,' said Sir Charles.

'No, I should suggest your coming by the later train. It's more convenient to meet you at the station.'

'Very well – as you like,' said he, inwardly a little astonished, as always at the easy working of the simple old plan, suggesting what one does not wish to do in order to be persuaded into what one does.

'And, by the way, I haven't heard you speak of Hyacinth lately. You had better go and see her. A little while ago you were always wasting your time about her, and I spoke to you about it, Charles – I think?'

'I think you did,' said he.

'But, though at one time I was growing simply tired of her name, I didn't mean that you need not look after her at *all*. Go and see her, and explain to her I can't possibly accompany you. Tell her I've got chronic lumbago very badly indeed, and I'm obliged to go to the country, but I shall certainly make a point of calling on her when I return. You won't forget, Charles?'

'Certainly not.'

'I should go oftener,' she continued apologetically, 'but I have such a great dislike to that companion of hers. I think Miss Yeo a most unpleasant person.'

'She isn't really,' said Sir Charles.

'I do wish we could get Hyacinth married,' said Lady Cannon. 'I know what a relief it would be to you, and it seems to me such an unheard-of thing for a young girl like that to be living practically alone!'

'We've been through that before, Janet. Remember, there was nothing else to do unless she continued to live with us. And as your nerves can't even stand Ella – '

Lady Cannon dropped the point.

'Well, we must get her married,' she said again.

'What a good thing Ella is still so young! Girls are a dreadful responsibility,' and she swept graciously from the dining-room.

Sir Charles took out an irritating little notebook of red leather, the sort of thing that is advertised when lost as 'of no value to anyone but the owner'. It was full of mysterious little marks and unintelligible little notes. He put down, in cabalistic signs, '*Hyacinth's dinner, eight o'clock.*' He enjoyed writing her name, even in hieroglyphics.

A proposal

'I SAY, Eugenia.'

  'Well, Cecil?'

 'Look here, Eugenia.'

 'What is it, Cecil?'

 'Will you marry me?'

 'I beg your pardon?'

 'Will you marry me, Eugenia?'

 '*What?*'

 'You heard what I said. I asked you to marry me. Will you?'

 '*Certainly* not! Most decidedly not! How can you ask such a ridiculous question!'

The lady who thus scornfully rejected a proposal was no longer young, and had never been beautiful. In what exactly her attraction consisted was perhaps a mystery to many of those who found themselves under the charm. Her voice and smile were very agreeable, and she had a graceful figure. If she looked nearly ten years younger than her age (which was forty-four), this was in no way owing to any artificial aid, but to a kind of brilliant vitality, not a bouncing mature liveliness, but a vivid, intense, humorous interest in life that was and would always remain absolutely fresh. She was naturalness itself, and seemed unconscious or careless of her appearance. Nor did she have that well-preserved air of so many modern women who seem younger than their years, but seemed merely clever, amiable, very unaffected, and rather ill. She had long, veiled-looking brown eyes, turned up at the corners, which gave to her glance an amusing slyness. It was a very misleading physiognomical effect, for she was really unusually frank. She wore a dull grey dress that was neither artistic, becoming, nor smart. In fact, she was too charming to be dowdy, and too careless to be chic; she might have been a great celebrity.

The young man who made the suggestion above recorded was fair and clean-shaven, tall and well-made, with clear-cut feature; in fact, he was very good-looking – good-looking as almost only an Englishman can be. Under a reserved, dandified manner, he tried unsuccessfully to conceal the fact that he was too intelligent for his type. He did not, however, quite attain his standard of entire expressionlessness; and his bright, light-blue eyes and fully-curved lips showed the generous and emotional nature of their owner. At this moment he seemed very much out of temper.

They were sitting in a dismal little drawing-room in one of the smallest houses in a dreary street in Belgravia. The room was crowded with dateless, unmeaning furniture, and disfigured by muddled, mistaken decoration. Its designer, probably, had meant well, but had been very far from carrying out his meaning. There were too many things in the room, and most of them were wrong. It would be unjust, however, to suppose Mrs Raymond did not know this. Want of means, and indifference, or perhaps perverseness, had caused her to leave the house unchanged since his death as a sort of monument to poor Colonel Raymond's erring taste.

'You might just as well marry me as not,' said Cecil, in his level voice, but with pleading eyes. He made the gesture of trying to take her hand, but she took hers away.

'You are very pressing, Cecil, but I think not. You know perfectly well – I'm sure I make no secret of it – that I'm ten years older than you. Old enough to be your mother! Am I the sort of person who would take advantage of the fancy of a gilded youth? And, now I come to think of it, your proposal's quite insulting. It's treating me like an adventuress! It's implying that you think I *would* marry you! Apologise, and withdraw it at once, or I'll never speak to you again.'

'This is nonsense. To begin with,' said Cecil, 'I may be a little gilded – not so very – but I'm far from being a youth. I'm thirty-four.'

'Yes, I know! That's just the absurd part,' she answered inconsequently. 'It's not as if you were a mere boy and didn't know better! And you know how I *hate* this sort of thing.'

'I know you do, and very likely I wouldn't have worried about marrying at all if you had been nicer to me – in other ways. You see, you brought it on yourself!'

'What *do* you mean? I *am* nice. Don't you come here whenever you like – or nearly? Didn't I dine with you once – a year or two ago? I forget, but I think I did.'

'You never did,' he answered sharply.

'Then it must have been with somebody else. Of course I didn't. I shouldn't dream of such a thing.'

'Someone else! Yes, of course; that's it. Well, I want you to marry me, Eugenia, because I want to get you away from everyone else. You see my point?'

She laughed. 'Oh, jealousy! That's the last straw. Do you know that you're a nuisance, Cecil?'

'Because I love you?' he said, trying to look into her sly Japanese eyes.

She avoided his glance.

'Because you keep on bothering. Always writing, always telephoning, always calling! As soon as I've disposed of *one* invitation or excuse to meet, you invent another. But this last idea is quite too exasperating.' She spoke more gently. 'Don't you know, Cecil, that I've been a widow for years? Would I be so ridiculous as to marry again? Why, the one thing I can't stand is being interfered with! I prefer, far prefer, being poor and alone to that. Now what I want you to do is to marry someone else. I have an idea who I should like it to be, but I won't talk about it now. It's the most charming girl in the world. I shan't tell you her name, that would be tactless. It's that lovely Miss Verney, of course. She's much too good for you – an heiress, a beauty, and an orphan! But she's wonderful; and she really deserves you.'

He stopped her.

'How heartless you are!' he said admiringly.

'Really not, Cecil. I'm very fond of you. I'd be your best friend if you'd let me, but I shan't speak to you again or receive you at all unless you promise not to repeat that nonsense about marrying. I know how horridly obstinate you are! Please remember it's out of the question.'

At this moment the servant brought in a letter to Mrs Raymond. As she read it, Cecil thought she changed colour.

'It's only a line from Sir Charles Cannon,' she said.

'What's he writing about?'

'Really, Cecil! What right have you to ask? I certainly shan't say. It's about his ward, if you must know. And now I think you'd better go, if you will make these violent scenes.'

He stood up.

'You must let me come soon again,' he said rather dejectedly. I'll try not to come tomorrow. Shall I?'

'Yes, do try – not to come, I mean. And will you do everything I tell you?'

'I suppose it will please you if I dine with Hyacinth Verney this evening? She asked me yesterday. I said I was half-engaged, but would let her know.'

'Yes, it *would* please me very much indeed,' said Mrs Raymond. 'Please do it, and try to know her better. She's sweet. I don't know her, but – '

'All right. If you'll be nice to me. Will you?'

She was reading the letter again, and did not answer when he said good-bye and left the room.

The little Ottleys

'EDITH, I want you to look nice tonight, dear; what are you going to wear?'

'My Other Dress,' said Edith.

'Is it all right?'

'It ought to be. Would you like to know what I've done to it? I've cut the point into a square, and taken four yards out of the skirt; the chiffon off my wedding-dress has been made into kimono sleeves; then I'm going to wear my wedding-veil as a sort of scarf thrown carelessly over the shoulders; and I've turned the pointed waist-band round, so that it's quite *right* and short-waisted at the back now, and – '

'Oh, don't tell me the horrible details! I think you might take a little interest in *me*. I thought of wearing a button-hole. Though you may have forgotten it now, before I was a dull old married man, I was supposed to dress rather well, Edith.'

'I know you were.'

'I thought I'd wear a white carnation.'

'I should wear two – one each side. It would be more striking.'

'That's right! Make fun of me! I hope you'll be ready in time. They dine at eight, you know.'

'Bruce, you're not going to begin to dress yet, are you? It's only just four.'

He pretended not to hear, and said peevishly –

'I suppose they don't expect *us* to ask *them?* I daresay it's well known we can't return all the hospitality we receive.'

'I daresay it is.'

'It's awful not having a valet,' said Bruce.

'But it would be more awful if we had,' said Edith. 'Where on earth could we put him – except in the bathroom?'

'I don't think you'll look you're best tonight,' he answered rather revengefully.

'Give me a chance! Wait till I've waved my hair!'

'He read the paper for a little while, occasionally reading aloud portions of it that she had already read, then complained that she took no interest in public events.

'What do you think Archie brought home today,' she said to change the subject, 'in his Noah's Ark? Two snails!' She laughed.

'Revolting! *I* don't know where he gets his tastes from. Not from *my* family, that I'm quite sure.' He yawned ostentatiously.

'I think I shall have a rest,' Bruce said presently. 'I had a very bad night last night. I scarcely slept at all.'

'Poor boy!' Edith said kindly. She was accustomed to the convention of Bruce's insomnia, and it would never have occurred to her to appear surprised when he said he hadn't closed his eyes, though she happened to know there was no cause for anxiety. If he woke up ten minutes before he was called, he thought he had been awake all night; if he didn't he saw symptoms of the sleeping sickness.

She arranged cushions on the sofa and pulled the blinds down. A minute later he turned on the electric light and began to read again. Then he turned it out, pulled up the blinds, and called her back.

'I want to speak to you about my friend Raggett,' he said seriously. 'I've asked him to dinner here tomorrow. What shall we have?'

'Oh, Bruce! Let's wait and settle tomorrow.'

'You don't know Raggett, but I think you'll like him. I *think* you will. In any case, there's no doubt Raggett's been remarkably decent to me. In fact, he's a very good sort.'

'Fancy!' said Edith.

'Why do you say fancy?' he asked irritably.

'I don't exactly know. I must say something. I'm sure he's nice if he's a friend of yours, dear.'

'He's a clever chap in his way. At least, when I say clever, I don't mean clever in the ordinary sense.'

'Oh, I see,' said Edith.

'He's very amusing,' continued Bruce. 'He said a very funny thing to me the other day. Very funny indeed. It's no use repeating it, because unless you knew all the circumstances and the *characters* of the people that he told the story of, you wouldn't see the point. Perhaps, after all, I'd better ask him to dine at the club.'

'Oh no! Let him come here. Don't you think I'm worthy to see Raggett?'

'Oh nonsense, dear, I'm very proud of you,' said Bruce kindly. 'It isn't exactly that. . . . Mind you, Raggett's quite a man of the world – and yet he *isn't* a man of the world, if you know what I mean.'

'I see,' said Edith again.

'I can't decide whether to ask him here or not,' said Bruce, walking up and down the room in agitation.

'Well, suppose we leave it till tomorrow. You can make up your mind then,' she said good-naturedly.

Edith was dressed, when she found Bruce still in the throes of an agitated toilet. Having lost his collar-stud, he sat down and gave himself up to cold despair.

'You go without me,' he said in a resigned voice. 'Explain the reason – no, don't explain it. Say I've got influenza – but then perhaps they'll think you ought to look after me, and – '

'Here it is!' said Edith.

In the cab he recovered suddenly, and told her she looked awfully pretty, which cheered her very much. She was feeling rather tired. She had spent several hours in the nursery that day, pretending to be a baby giraffe with so much success that Archie had insisted upon countless encores, until, like all artists who have to repeat the same part too often, she felt the performance was becoming mechanical.

Hyacinth's little dinner

'THE little Ottleys', as they were called (they were a tall, fine-looking couple), found themselves in a small circle of people who were all most pleasing to the eye, with the single exception of Miss Yeo. And even she, in a markedly elegant dress of a peculiarly vicious shade of green, had her value in the picture. A little shocked by the harshness of the colour, one's glance turned with relief to Hyacinth, in satin of a blue so pale that it looked like the reflection of the sky in water. A broad, pale blue ribbon was wound in and out of her brown hair in the Romney fashion. Of course she looked her best. Women always do if they wish to please one man when others are there, and she was in the slightly exalted frame of mind that her reflection in the mirror had naturally given her.

The faint atmosphere of chaperonage that always hung about Sir Charles in Hyacinth's house did not interfere with his personal air of enjoying an escapade, nor with his looking distinguished to the very verge of absurdity. As to Cecil, the reaction from his disappointment of the afternoon had made him look more vivid than usual. He was flushed with failure.

He talked rather irresponsibly, and looked at Hyacinth, his neighbour at dinner, with such obvious appreciation, that her gaiety became infectious. In the little panelled dining-room which, like all the house, was neither commonplace nor bizarre, but simple and distinguished, floated an atmosphere of delightful ease and intimacy.

Sir Charles admired the red roses, which Anne declared she had bought for two-and-threepence.

'Very ingenious,' said Sir Charles.

'I *am* ingenious and clever,' said Anne. 'I get my cleverness from my father, and my economy from my mother. My father's a clergyman, but his wife was a little country girl – a sort of Merry Peasant; like Schumann's piece, you know. Peasants are always merry.'

'I fancy that's a myth,' said Cecil. 'If not, I've been singularly unfortunate, for all the peasants *I* ever ran across seemed most depressed.'

'Of course, if you ran over them!' said Hyacinth.

'But I didn't exactly run over them; I only asked them the way to somewhere. They *were* angry! Now I come to think of it, though, they weren't peasants at all. It was only one man. He was a shepherd. I got to know him better afterwards, and he was rather a good chap. Shepherds don't have a bad time; they just wear ribbons and crooks and dance with shepherdesses, you know.'

'Oh, then *can* you tell me why a red sky at night is a shepherd's delight?' asked Hyacinth. 'Is it because it's a sign of rain, and he needn't look after the sheep, but can go fast asleep like little Bo-peep – or was it little Boy Blue – if he likes?'

'For you, I'll try to find out; but I'm ashamed to say I know very little of natural history – or machinery, or lots of other interesting things. And, what's far worse, I don't even want to know any more. I like to think there are some mysteries left in life.'

'I quite agree with you that it would be rather horrid to know exactly how electricity works, and how trains go, and all that sort of thing. I like some things just to *happen*. I never broke my dolls to see what they were made of. I had them taken away the *moment* any sawdust began to come out,' said Hyacinth.

'You were perfectly right, Miss Verney. You're an Idealist; at least, you don't like practical details. But still you take a great interest in other people psychologically. You want to know, I'm sure, just how a shepherd really feels, and why he feels it. I don't even care for that, and I'm not very keen on scenery, or places either, or even things. My Uncle Ted's so frightfully fond of Things. He's a collector, you know, and I don't sympathise a bit. In fact, I hate things.'

'You seem rather difficult to please, Mr Reeve. What *do* you like?'

'People; at least, some people. Don't you?'

'Do you like people who talk nonsense?'

'Yes, and still more people who listen to it charmingly,' he answered. 'I didn't know before tonight that you ever listened to nonsense or talked it. I always thought you were the person who solves all the Hard Cases in *Vanity Fair* - under different names.'

'I wonder you didn't think I won all the prizes in the Limericks,' said Hyacinth.

'I have my faults, Miss Verney, but I'm not blasphemous. Will you have an olive?'

She accepted it. He lowered his voice to say –

'How wonderful you're looking tonight!'

'What am I to say to that? I don't think people should make unanswerable remarks at dinner,' she said, trying to look reproving, but turning pink with pleasure.

'If people will look adorable at dinner – or anywhere – they must take the consequences,' said Cecil, under cover of a very animated discussion between Bruce and Miss Yeo on sixpenny cab-fares.

Then for a second he felt a remorseful twinge of disloyalty. But that was nonsense; wasn't he obeying Mrs Raymond's distinct commands? Nothing would please her so much . . .

And to flirt with Hyacinth was not at all a disagreeable task. He reflected that Eugenia might have asked him to do something a good deal harder.

Under the combined influence, then, of duty, pique, and a little champagne, he gave way to the curious fascination that Hyacinth had always had for him, and she was only too ready to be happy.

He remembered how he had first met her. He had been dragged to the Burlingtons' dance – he loathed all large parties – and, looking drearily round, he'd been struck by, and asked to be introduced to, Miss Verney. She wasn't Eugenia, of course, and could never, he was sure, be part of his life. He thought that Eugenia appealed to his better nature and to his intellect.

He felt even a little ashamed of the purely sensuous attraction Hyacinth possessed for him, while he was secretly very proud of being in love with Mrs Raymond. Not everyone would appreciate Eugenia! Cecil was still young enough to wish to *be* different from other people, while desiring still more, like all Englishmen, to *appear* as much as possible like everybody else.

He did not thoroughly understand Hyacinth; he couldn't quite place her. She was certainly not the colourless *jeune fille* idealised by the French, but she had even less of the hard abruptness of the ordinary young unmarried Englishwoman. She called herself a bachelor girl, but hadn't the touch of the Bohemian that phrase usually seems to imply. She was too plastic, too finished. He admired her social dexterity, her perfect harmony with the charming background she had so well arranged for herself. Yet, he thought, for such a young girl, only twenty-two, she was too complex, too civilised. Mrs Raymond, for instance, seemed much more downright and careless. He was growing somewhat bewildered between his analysis of her character and his admiration for her mouth, an admiration that was rather difficult to keep entirely cool and theoretical, and that he felt a strong inclination to show in some more practical manner. . . . With a sigh he turned to Edith Ottley, his other neighbour.

As soon as Anne had locked up she removed with the greatest care her emerald dress, which she grudged wearing a second longer than was necessary, and put on an extraordinary dressing-gown of which it was hardly too much to say that there was probably not another one exactly like it in Europe. Hyacinth always said it had been made out of an old curtain from the Rev Mr Yeo's library in the Devonshire Rectory, and Anne did not deny it.

She then screwed up her hair into a tight knot, put one small piece of it into a curling pin, which she then pinned far back on her head (as if afraid that the effect on the forehead would be too becoming), took off her dainty green shoes, put on an enormous pair of grotesque slippers, carpet slippers (also a relic), and went into Hyacinth's room. Anne made it a rule every evening to go in for a few minutes to see Hyacinth and talk against everyone they had seen during the day. She seemed to regard it as a sacred duty, almost like saying her prayers. Hyacinth sometimes professed to find this custom a nuisance, but she would certainly have missed it. Tonight she was smiling happily to herself, and took no notice of Anne's entrance.

'I suppose you think it went off well,' said Anne aggressively.

'Didn't it?'

'I thought the dinner was ridiculous. A young girl like you asking two or three friends needn't have a banquet fit for a Colonial Conference. Besides, the cook lost her head. She sent up the same dish twice.'

'Did she? How funny! How was that?'

'Of course, *you* wouldn't know. She and the kitchenmaid were playing Diabolo till the last minute in the housekeeper's room. However, you needn't worry; nobody noticed it.'

'That's all right. Didn't Edith look pretty?'

Anne poked the fire spitefully.

'Like the outside of a cheap chocolate-box.'

'Oh, Anne, what nonsense! Bruce seemed irritable, and fatuous. I didn't envy Edith going back with him.'

'Bruce was jealous of Cecil Reeve, of course. You hardly looked at anybody else.'

'Anne, really tonight there were one or two little things that made me think he is beginning to like me. I don't say he's perfect; I daresay he has his faults. But there's something I like about his face. I wonder what it is.'

'I know what it is, he's very good-looking,' said Anne.

'Do you think he cares for me?'

'No, I don't.'

'Oh, Anne!'

'I think, perhaps, he will, in time – in a way.'

'Do you think if I were very careful not to show I liked him it would be better?'

'No, there's only one chance for you.'

'What is it?'

'Keep on hammering.'

'*Indeed* I shan't! I never heard of such a thing. I suppose you think there's somebody else?' said Hyacinth, sitting up angrily.

'Oh, I daresay he's just finishing off with someone or other, and you may catch him on the rebound.'

'What horrid things you say!'

'I only say what I think,' said Anne. 'Anyhow, you had a success tonight, I could see, because poor Charles seemed so depressed. Why do you have all these electric lights burning when one lamp would be enough?'

'Oh, go away, Anne, and don't bother,' said Hyacinth, laughing.

On his return home, Cecil suddenly felt a violent reaction in favour of Mrs Raymond. Certainly he had enjoyed his evening with Hyacinth, but it was very bitter to him to think what pleasure that enjoyment would have given to Eugenia. . . . He began to think he couldn't live without her. Something must be done. Further efforts must be made. The idea struck him that he would go and see his uncle, Lord Selsey, about it. He knew Uncle Ted was really fond of him, and wouldn't like to see his life ruined (so he put it to himself), and his heart broken, though he also probably would disapprove from the worldly point of view. Decidedly unhappy, yet to a certain extent enjoying his misery, Cecil went to sleep.

Lord Selsey

THE mere thought of confiding in Lord Selsey was at once soothing and bracing. He was a widower with no children, and Cecil was by way of being his heir. Since the death of his wife he lived in a kind of cultured retirement in a large old house standing a little by itself in Cambridge Gate. He used to declare that this situation combined all the advantages of London and the country, also that the Park that was good enough for the Regent was good enough for him. He had a decided cult for George IV; and there was even more than a hint of Beau Brummel in his dress. The only ugly thing in the house was a large coloured print of the pavilion at Brighton.

In many ways Lord Selsey was Cecil's model; and unconsciously, in his uncle's suave presence, the young man's manner always became more expressive and his face more inscrutable.

Lord Selsey was remarkably handsome; the even profile, well-shaped head, and blond colouring were much the same in uncle and nephew, the uncle's face having, perhaps, a more idealistic cast. The twenty years' difference in age had only given the elder man a finer, fairer, more faded look, and the smooth light hair, still thick, was growing grey.

Cecil was not surprised to find his uncle sitting in his smoking-room, smoking, and not reading the morning paper. He was looking over his collection of old coins. At a glance he saw by Cecil's excessive quietness that the boy, as he called him, was perturbed, so he talked about the coins for some minutes.

Cecil made little attempt to conceal that fact that Things bored him.

'Well, what is it?' said Lord Selsey abruptly.

Cecil couldn't think of anything better by way of introducing the trouble than the vaguely pessimistic statement that everything was rather rotten.

'You don't gamble, you're not even very hard up. . . . It's a woman, of course,' said Lord Selsey, 'and you want to marry, I suppose, or you wouldn't come to me about it. . . . Who is she?'

Cecil gave a rough yet iridescent sketch of Mrs Raymond.

'Of course she's older than I am, but it doesn't make the slightest difference. She's been a widow ever since she was twenty. She's very hard up, and she doesn't care. She's refused me, but I want to make her come round. . . . No, she isn't *pretty*, not very.'

Lord Selsey put his old coins away, and leant back in his chair.

'I should like to see her,' he said thoughtfully.

'I'm sure of one thing, uncle you could never have any vulgar, commonplace ideas about her – I mean, she's so *peculiarly* disinterested, and all that sort of thing. You mustn't fancy she's a dangerous siren, don't you know, or. . . . For instance, she doesn't care much for dress; she just sticks up her hair anyhow, and parts it in the middle.'

'Then it would certainly be difficult to believe anything against her,' said Lord Selsey.

'Besides, she really wants me to marry someone else.'

'Who?'

'She's always trying to persuade me to propose to Hyacinth Verney ... you know, that pretty girl, old Cannon's ward. . . . She *is* awfully pretty, of course, I know.'

'I should like to see her,' said Lord Selsey.

Cecil smiled. It was well known that Lord Selsey was a collector. Though no-one could have less of the pompous, fatuous vanity of the Don Juan, beauty had always played, and always would play, a very prominent part in his life. It was, in fact, without exception, his greatest pleasure, and interest – even passion. The temperament that gave to beauty and charm a rather inordinate value had, no doubt, descended to his nephew. But Cecil was, in that as in everything else, much less of a dilettante.

'You actually want me to advise you to persuade Mrs Raymond to marry you? My dear boy, how can I?'

'How is it you don't say she's quite right not to?' asked Cecil curiously.

'From her point of view I think she's quite wrong. As you're both practically free and you would marry her tomorrow – or this afternoon for choice – if she cared for you she would probably do it. Where I think she's wrong is in *not* caring for you. . . . Who is it?'

'I don't believe it's anyone. Eugenia's peculiar; she's very independent, very fantastic. She likes to do whatever comes into her head. She's very fascinating ... but I shouldn't be at all surprised if she's absolutely cold; I mean, really never could care for any man at all.'

'I *should* like to see her,' repeated Lord Selsey, his eyes brightening.

'It's most awfully good of you, Uncle, the way you take it. I mean to say, I'm afraid I'm not at all asking your consent, you know, or anything of that sort, as I ought.'

'You're asking my advice, and it's about the only thing most men of my age enjoy giving. Well, really, Cecil, and frankly, I think it's a dismal little story. It would be humbug if I pretended I was sorry about Mrs Raymond's – a – attitude, and I quite see its absolute genuineness. But, if you'll excuse my saying so, what price the other girl?'

'What price? No price.'

'*She* likes you,' said Lord Selsey acutely.

'What makes you think that?'

'Because otherwise you wouldn't be so cool about her. You're a little too frightened of being obvious, Cecil. I was like that, too. But don't give way to it. Hyacinth Verney – what a charming name! ... What would old Cannon say?'

'I don't think he seems particularly keen on *me*,' said Cecil frankly.

'That's odd. Then he must be very ambitious for her, or else be in love with her himself ... probably both.'

'Oh, I say, Uncle Ted! Why, there's Lady Cannon! She's a very handsome, gigantic woman, and they have a daughter of their own, a girl called Ella, at school in Paris. She's pretty, too, only a flapper, you know, with a fair plait and a black bow.'

'I should like to see her; what delightful families you get yourself mixed up with, Cecil! If I were you I should certainly cultivate the Verney girl. I know it's no use telling you to do the contrary, as I should if you weren't in your present frame of mind.'

'I should *very* much like you to meet Eugenia,' said Cecil.

'Yes. How shall we arrange it? A dinner at the Savoy or something?'

'No. Somehow that isn't the kind of thing she'd like,' said Cecil.

'I thought not. But if I suddenly go and call on her, even with you, wouldn't it make it too much of a family affair? And I should be so afraid of having the air of trying to persuade her to give you up. I don't want to make a fool of myself, you know.'

Cecil seemed a little stung, though he smiled.

'If she knew *you*, perhaps it would make her more interested in me!'

'Do you think she'd come and hear some music here,' said Lord Selsey, 'if I wrote and asked her?'

'Yes, I think she might. There's no nonsense about her – about etiquette and things of that sort, I mean.'

'Then that's settled. You tell her about it, and I'll write. On Thursday afternoon. The two young pianists, George Ranger and Nevil Butt, are coming, and the little girl, the new Russian singer.'

'A juvenile party?' asked Cecil, laughing.

'No, only two or three people.'

'Two or three hundred, I suppose. Well, I'll get Mrs Raymond to come. Thanks so much.'

They shook hands with more than cordiality. As Cecil went out his uncle said –

'You've been most interesting this morning. But the other girl's the one, you know. Don't neglect her.'

He laughed, for he saw the young man was rather flattered at the notion. Evidently, Mrs Raymond was worth knowing.

The peculiarities of Raggett

'OH, Bruce,' said Edith, as she looked up from a Sale Catalogue, 'I do wish you would be an angel and let me have a little cash to go to Naylor and Rope's. There are some marvellous bargains – spring novelties – there, and Archie absolutely *needs* one or two things.'

Bruce frowned and sat down to breakfast, rather heavily.

'I object,' he said as he took his coffee, 'on principle – purely on principle – to spring sales. Women buy a lot of things they don't want, and ruin their husbands under the ridiculous impression they're buying bargains.'

'I won't ruin you, dear. I want to get Archie a coat – and a hat. I only want ' – she watched his expression – ' a sovereign – or two.' She smiled brightly, and passed him the toast.

His manner softened.

'Well, dear, you know I'm not a rich man, don't you?'

'Yes, dear.'

'But I should much prefer that you should get Archie's things at a first-rate place like Wears and Swells, where we have an account, and send me the bill. Will you do that?'

'Of course I will, if you like; but it'll cost more.'

She had often marvelled at a comparative lavishness about cheques that Bruce combined with a curious loathing to parting from any coin, however small.

'Then that's settled. And now I want to speak to you about Raggett.'

He paused, and then said seriously, 'I've absolutely decided and very nearly made up my mind to have Raggett to dinner tonight at the Savoy.'

'The Savoy?'

'Yes, yes; no doubt this little flat is very comfortable' – he looked round the room with marked disdain – 'and cook, thanks to you, isn't half *bad* . . . but one can't give *dinners* here! And after all I've said to Raggett – oh, one thing and another – I fancy I've given him the impression of a rather luxurious home. It won't matter if he calls here in the afternoon some day, but for a man like that, I'd rather – yes – the Savoy. You look as if you objected. Do you?'

'Not at all. It'll be rather fun. But I'm so glad you can afford it. We haven't an *account* there, you know.'

'I propose to make a slight sacrifice for once. . . . I will engage a table and telephone to Raggett. Women never understand that to do things well, once in a way, is sometimes a – a very good thing,' he finished rather lamely.

'All right. I *am* getting curious to see Raggett!'

'My dear Edith, he's nothing particular to *see*, but he's a man who might be – very useful.'

'Oh, shall you take a private room?'

'I don't think so. Why? You can wear what you wore last night. . . . You looked quite nice in it, and you can take it from me, once for all' – he got up, looked in the glass, and said – 'that *Raggett's all right*. Now, tell cook we're dining out. She might have a holiday tonight. A change may do her good; and I shall hope to find the omelette less leathery tomorrow.'

Edith did not point out that Bruce, after specially ordering breakfast punctually at nine, had come down at half-past ten.

'And now I must go.... The dinner was charming last night. It was only spoilt by that empty-headed fool – what's his name – Reeve, who was obviously making up to Hyacinth. Anyone can see she only endures his attentions from politeness, of course. He knows nothing about anything. I found *that* out when we were smoking after dinner; and one can't get a word out of old Cannon.'

Edith was putting Bruce's writing-table in order when she found an open letter in the blotting-book, glanced at the signature, and saw that it was from Raggett. So she eagerly read it, hoping to get some further light on the mysterious man in whose honour Bruce was prepared to offer so extravagant a festivity.

It was written on a rough sheet of paper, with no address. The handwriting was small, compressed, and very untidy. It ran –

DEAR OTTLEY,

Y'rs to hand. I shall be glad to dine with you, as I have told you several times, and I would accept your invitation with pleasure if I knew when and where the dinner was to be. These two points you have always avoided mentioning.

Y'rs truly,

J. R. RAGGETT

It struck Edith that it was quite extraordinary, after so many descriptions from Bruce – some vivid, some sketchy, others subtly suggestive – how little she could imagine Raggett.

Notwithstanding quantities of words, nothing, somehow, had ever come out to throw the least glimmer of light either on his character, personality, or walk of life. Not bad, all right, useful, rather wonderful, but quite ordinary and nothing particular, were some of the phrases she recalled. She had never been told anything about his age, nor his appearance, nor how long Bruce had known him. She had only gathered that he wasn't athletic like Goldthorpe (Bruce's golf companion), and that he wasn't in the Foreign Office, and didn't belong to Bruce's club. Where, how, and when could he be useful?

If she seemed bored when Bruce was enthusiastic about him, he was offended; but if she seemed interested and asked leading questions, he became touchy and cautious, almost jealous. Sometimes she had begun to think that Raggett was a Mrs Harris - that there was no such person. There, evidently, she had been wrong.

At eight o'clock that evening, on arriving at the Savoy, Edith decided not to take off her cloak (on the ground of chilliness, but really because it was smarter and more becoming than her dress). Therefore she waited in the outer room while Bruce, who seemed greatly excited, and had given her various contradictory tips about how to behave to their guest, was taking off his coat. Several other people were waiting there. She saw herself in the glass - a pretty, fair, typically Engish-looking woman, with neatly-chiselled features, well-arranged *blond-cendré* hair, a tall, slight figure, and a very thin neck. She noticed, among the other people waiting, a shabby-looking man of about thirty-five, who looked so intensely uncomfortable that she pitied him. He had a vague, rough, drab beard, colourless hair, which was very thick in front and very thin at the back, quite indefinite features, an undecided expression, and the most extraordinary clothes she had ever seen. The shirt-front was soft, and was in large bulging pleats. He wore an abnormal-looking big black tie, and the rest of the costume suggested a conjurer who had arrived at a children's party in the country and had forgotten his dress-suit, and borrowed various portions of it from different people staying in the house, who were either taller or shorter than himself. The waistcoat ended too soon, and the coat began too late; the collar reminded one of Gladstone; while the buttonhole of orchids (placed, rather eccentrically, very low down on the coat) completed the general effect of political broadmindedness, combined with acute social anxiety.

He looked several times at Edith with a furtive but undisguised admiration. Then Bruce appeared, held out his hand cordially, and said, 'Ah, Raggett, here you are!'

A musical afternoon

LORD SELSEY often said he disapproved of the ordinary sub-divisions of a house, and, especially as he lived alone, he did not see why one should breakfast in a breakfast-room, dine in a dining-room, draw in a drawing-room, and so on. Nevertheless, he had one special room for music. There was a little platform at the end of it, and no curtains or draperies of any kind to obscure or stifle sound. A frieze of Greek figures playing various instruments ran round the walls, which were perfectly plain so that nothing should distract the eye from the pleasures of the ear; but he was careful to avoid that look of a concert-room given by rows of chairs (suggesting restraint and reserved guinea seats), and the music-room was furnished with comfortable lounges and led into a hall containing small Empire sofas, in which not more than two persons could be seated. Therefore the audience at his entertainments often enjoyed themselves almost as much as the performers, which is rare.

This afternoon there was the usual number of very tall women in large highly-decorated hats, smooth-haired young men in coats that went in at the waist, a very few serious amateurs with longish hair, whose appearance did not quite come up to the standard of the *Tailor and Cutter*, and a small number of wistful professional feminine artists in no collars and pince-nez – in fact, the average fashionable, artistic crowd. The two young geniuses, George Ranger and Nevil Butt, had just given their rather electrifying performance, one playing the compositions of the other, and then both singing Fauré together, and a small band of Green Bulgarians were now playing strenuously a symphony of Richard Strauss, when Cecil and Mrs Raymond appeared together. Lord Selsey received her as if she had been an old friend. When they shook hands they felt at once, after one glance at Cecil and then at each other, that they were more than friends – they were almost accomplices.

By one of those fortunate social accidents that are always occurring in London, Lord Selsey had met Hyacinth and Anne Yeo at a party the day before, had been introduced to them, and invited them to hear Ranger and Butt. Hyacinth, aware she was to meet Mrs Raymond, wore her loveliest clothes and sweetest expression, though she could not keep out of her eyes a certain anxiety, especially when she saw that Cecil greeted her with a slight, cold embarrassment that was very different from his usual manner. He had not expected to meet Hyacinth, and resolved to avoid the introduction he knew she desired. But no man is a match for a woman in a detail of this sort. In the refreshment-room, where Cecil was pressing coffee on Mrs Raymond, Hyacinth walked in, accompanied by Anne, and stood not very far from him. He came up to her, as Hyacinth saw, at Mrs Raymond's instigation.

'Can I get you anything, Miss Verney? Some tea?'

'Thanks, yes. Isn't that Mrs Raymond? I do wish you would introduce me to her.'

Mrs Raymond came forward. Cecil murmured their names. They shook hands. Mrs Raymond looked at her with such impulsive admiration that she dropped a piece of cake. They spoke a few words about the music, and Cecil moved aside.

Anne called him back, not wishing to see him spared anything.

'You mustn't,' said Cecil, 'on any account miss the next thing. It is the wonderful new singer, don't you know - the little girl, Vera Schakoffsky.'

'Oh, very well,' said Hyacinth. 'I'll go,' and she went on with Anne. But when they had returned to the music-room she said to Anne, 'I left my handkerchief,' and went back to the refreshment-room.

A screen was by the door. Just before she had passed it she heard Mrs Raymond say -

'What an angel! How can you not be at her feet? Go and talk to her at once, or I'll never speak to you again!'

'I just shan't!' said Cecil doggedly. 'You make me simply ridiculous. If you won't be nice to me yourself, you needn't throw me at the head of other people.'

Hyacinth turned back and went to the music-room again.

Some time afterwards Cecil joined her, Mrs Raymond having apparently disappeared. The new tenor was singing an old song. Cecil sat down next to Hyacinth on a little Empire sofa.

'Let me look at the programme,' he said. And as he took it from her he pressed her fingers. She snatched her hand angrily away.

'Pray don't do that,' she said in a contemptuous tone. 'Even to obey Mrs Raymond, you needn't do violence to your feelings!'

'Miss Verney! I beg your pardon! But what *do* you mean?'

'Surely you understand. And don't trouble to come and see me any more.'

He looked at her. Her suave social dexterity had vanished. Her eyes were dark with purely human instinctive jealousy. They looked at each other a moment, then Lord Selsey came up and said –

'I'm afraid my attempt at originality hasn't been quite a success. The concert's not as harmonious as I hoped. Come and have tea, Miss Verney.'

Hyacinth did not speak a word to Anne on their way home, nor did she refer to the afternoon, nor answer any remark of Anne's on the subject till that evening, when Anne came into her room to complain of the electric light and make fun of Lord Selsey's guests. Then she found Hyacinth sobbing, and saying –

'I shall get over it. I shall be all right tomorrow. I'm going to cut him out of my life!'

'He'll soon cut in again,' said Anne.

'Indeed he won't! I'm not going to be played with. Preferring an old Japanese who doesn't even *like* him, and then making a fool of me!'

'If she ran after him, and you begged him to stick to her, it would be the other way,' said Anne.

'What do you mean? Hasn't he any real preference?'

'Yes. He's attached to her, fond of her. She's utterly indifferent about him, so he's piqued. So he thinks that's being in love.'

'Then why does he try to deceive me and flirt with me at all?'

'He doesn't. You really attract him; you're suited to him physically and socially, perhaps mentally too. The suitability is so obvious that he doesn't like it. It's his feeling for you that he fights against, and especially because he sees you care for him.'

'I was horrid enough to him today! I told him never to call here again.'

'To show your indifference?'

'I made him understand that I wanted no more of his silly flirtation,' said Hyacinth, still tearful.

'If you *really* made him think that, everything will be all right.'

'Really, Anne, you're clever. I think I shall take your advice.'

Anne gave a queer laugh.

'I didn't know I'd given any, but I will. Whatever he does now, leave him alone!'

'I should think so! Then why did you tell me the other day to keep on hammering?'

'I was quite right the other day.'

'Didn't I look nicer than Mrs Raymond?'

'That's not the point. You talk as if you were rivals on the same platform. She's on a different plane. But he'll get tired in the end of her indifference and remember *you*,' added Anne sardonically.

'Then he'll find I've forgotten *him*. Oh, why am I so unhappy?'

'You're too emotional, but you'll be happy through that too. Please don't make your eyes red. There are other people in the world. Cecil Reeve – '

'And yet there's something so fascinating about him. He's so unlike anybody else.'

'Bosh!' said Anne. 'He's exactly like thousands of other young men. But it just happens you've taken a fancy to him; that's the only thing that makes him different.'

'I hate him,' said Hyacinth. 'Do you dislike him, Anne?'

'Dislike him?' said Anne, turning out one of the lights. 'No, indeed! I loathe him!'

'But why?'

Anne went to the door.

'Because you're a fool about him,' she said somewhat cryptically.

Hyacinth felt somewhat soothed, and resolved to think no more of Cecil Reeve. She then turned up the light again, took her writing materials, and wrote him three long letters, each of which she tore up. She then wrote once more, saying –

DEAR MR REEVE,

I shall be at home today at four. Do come round and see me.

She put it under her pillow, resolving to send it by a messenger the first thing in the morning, and went to sleep.

But this letter, like the others, was never sent. By the morning light she marvelled at having written it, and threw it into the fire.

The troubles of the Ottleys

'BRUCE,' said Edith, 'you won't forget we're dining with your people tonight?'

'It's a great nuisance.'

'Oh, Bruce!'

'It's such an infernally long way.'

'It's only to Kensington.'

'West Kensington. It's off the map. I'm not an explorer – I don't pretend to be.' He paused a moment, then went on, 'And it's not only the frightful distance and the expense of getting there, but when I *do* get there. . . . Do you consider that my people treat me with proper deference?'

'With proper *what?*' asked Edith.

'Deference. I admit I like deference. I need it – I require it; and at my people's – well, frankly, I don't get it.'

'If you need it,' said Edith, 'I hope you will get it. But remember they are your father and mother.'

'What do you mean by that?'

'Well, I mean they know you very well, of course . . . and all that.'

'Do you imply . . . ?'

'Oh, no, Bruce dear,' she answered hastily; 'of course I don't. But really I think your people are charming.'

'To *you* I know they are,' said he. 'It's all very well for you. They are awfully fond of *you*. You and my mother can talk about Archie and his nurse and housekeeping and fashions, and it's very jolly for you, but where's the fun for a man of the world?'

'Your father – ' began Edith.

'My father!' Bruce took a turn round the room. 'I don't mind telling you, Edith, I don't consider my father a man of the world. Why, good heavens! when we are alone together, what do you suppose he talks about? He complains! Finds fault, if you please! Says I don't work – makes out I'm extravagant! Have *you* ever found me extravagant?'

'No, indeed. I'm sure you've never been extravagant – to *me*.'

'He's not on my level intellectually in any way. I doubt very much if he's capable of understanding me at all. Still, I suppose we might as well go and get it over. My people's dinners are a most awful bore to me.'

'How would you like it,' said Edith gently, 'if some day Archie were to call us my people, and talk about us as you do of yours?'

'Archie!' shouted Bruce. 'Good heavens! Archie!' Bruce held out his arm with a magnificent gesture. 'If Archie ever treats me with any want of proper deference, I shall cut him off with a shilling!'

'Do give me the shilling for him now,' said Edith laughing.

The elder Mrs Ottley was a sweet woman, with a resigned smile and a sense of humour. She had a great admiration for Edith, who was very fond of her. No-one else was there on this occasion. Bruce always complained equally, regarding it as a slight if they were asked alone, and a bore if it was a dinner party. The elder Mr Ottley was considerably older than his wife, and was a handsome, clean-shaven elderly man with a hooked nose and a dry manner. The conversation at dinner consisted of vague attempts on Bruce's part to talk airy generalities, which were always brought back by his father to personalities more or less unflattering to Bruce.

Edith and Mrs Ottley, fearing an explosion, which happened rather frequently when Bruce and his father were together, combined their united energy to ward it off.

'And what do you intend the boy to be when he grows up?' asked old Mr Ottley. 'Are you going to make him a useful member of society, or a Foreign Office clerk?'

'I intend my son,' said Bruce – '(a little port, please. Thanks) – I intend my son to be a Man of the World.'

His father gave a slight snort.

'Be very careful,' said Mrs Ottley to Edith, 'not to let the darling catch cold in his perambulator this weather. Spring is so treacherous!'

'Does he seem to show any particular bent for anything? I suppose hardly – yet?'

'Well, he's very fond of soldiers,' said Edith.

'Ah!' said Mr Ottley approvingly; 'what we want for empire-building is conscription. Every fellow ought to be a soldier some time in his life. It makes men of them' – he glanced round rather contemptuously – 'it teaches them discipline.'

'I don't mean,' said Edith hastily, 'that he wants to *be* a soldier. But he likes playing with them. He takes them to bed with him. It is as much as I can do to keep him from eating them.'

'The angel!' said Mrs Ottley.

'You must be careful about that, Edith,' said Bruce solemnly. 'I understand red paint is poisonous.'

'It won't hurt him,' said old Mr Ottley, purely from a spirit of contradiction.

'But he's just as fond of animals,' said Edith quickly, to avert a storm. 'That Noah's Ark you gave him is his greatest pleasure. He's always putting the animals in and taking them out again.'

'Oh, the clever darling!' cried Mrs Ottley. 'You'd hardly believe it, Edith, but Bruce was like that when he was a little boy too. He used to – '

'Oh mother, do shut up!' said Bruce shame-facedly.

'Well, he was very clever,' said Mrs Ottley defiantly. 'You'd hardly think so now perhaps, but the things that child used to say!'

'Don't spoil Archie as his mother spoilt Bruce,' said Mr Ottley.

'Have you seen the new play at His Majesty's?' asked Bruce.

'No, I haven't. I went to the theatre *last* year,' said old Mr Ottley. '*I* haven't heaps of money to spend on superfluous amusements.'

'Bruce, you're not eating anything,' said Mrs Ottley anxiously. 'Do try some of these almonds and raisins. They're so good! I always get almonds and raisins at Harrod's now.'

Edith seemed much interested, and warmly assented to the simple proposition that they were the best almonds and raisins in the world.

The ladies retired.

'Most trying Mr Ottley's been lately,' said Mrs Ottley. 'Extremely worrying. Do you suppose I have had a single instant to go and order a new bonnet? Not a second! Has Bruce been tiresome at all?'

'Oh, no, he doesn't mean to be,' said Edith.

Mrs Ottley pressed her hand. 'Darling! I *know* what it is. What a sweet dress! You have the most perfect taste. I don't care what people say, those Empire dresses are most trying. I think you're so right not to give in to it as so many young women are doing. Fashion indeed! Hiding your waist under a bushel instead of being humbly thankful that you've got one! Archie is the sweetest darling. I see very little likeness to Bruce, or his father. I think he takes after *my* family, with a great look of you, dear. Most unfortunately, his father thinks Bruce is a little selfish . . . too fond of pleasure. But he's a great deal at home, isn't he, dear?'

'Yes, indeed,' said Edith, with a slight sigh. 'I think it's only that he's always been a little bit spoilt. No wonder, the only son! But he's a great dear, really.'

His mother shook her head. 'Dear loyal girl! I used to be like that too. May I give you a slight hint? Never contradict. Never oppose him. Agree with him, then he'll change his mind; or if he doesn't, say you'll do as he wishes, and act afterwards in the matter as your own judgement dictates. He'll never find it out. What's that?'

A door banged, hasty steps were heard. Bruce came into the drawing-room alone, looking slightly flushed and agitated.

'Where's your father?' asked Mrs Ottley.

'Gone to his study. . . . We'd better be getting home, Edith.'

Edith and Mrs Ottley exchanged glances. They had not been able to prevent the explosion after all.

At the National Gallery

IT was with considerable difficulty and self-restraint that Cecil succeeded in waiting till the next day to see Mrs Raymond after his uncle's party. He was of an age and of a temperament that made his love affairs seem to him supremely urgent and of more importance than anything else in his life.

He called on Mrs Raymond at eleven in the morning on the pretext of having something important to tell her. He found her sitting at her writing-table in a kind of red kimono. Her hair was brushed straight off her forehead, her eyes were sly and bright, and she looked more Japanese than ever.

Cecil told her what Hyacinth had said to him.

'Now, you see, I *can't* go on making up to her any more. She doesn't care a straw about me, and she sees through it, of course. I've done what you asked me. Won't you be nice to me now?'

'Certainly not! She's quite devoted to you. Telling you not to go and see her again! I never heard of anything so encouraging in my life. Now, Cecil,' she spoke seriously, 'that girl is a rare treasure. It's not only that she's a perfect beauty, but I read her soul yesterday. She has a beautiful nature, and she's in love with you. You don't appreciate her. If you take what she said literally, you're much stupider than I gave you credit for being. I - I simply shan't see you again till you've made it up. When you know her better you *must* care for her. Besides, I insist upon it. If you don't - well, you'll have to turn your attention somewhere else. For I seriously mean it. I won't see you.'

He looked obstinate.

'It's a fad of yours, Eugenia.'

'It's not a fad of mine. It's an opportunity of yours - one that you're throwing away in the most foolish way, that you might regret all your life. At any rate, *I'm* not going to be the cause of giving that poor darling another moment's annoyance or uneasiness. The idea of the angelic creature being worried about *me*! Why, it's preposterous! I'm sure she heard what I said to you when she came in behind the screen. I can't bear it, and I won't have it. Now go and see her, and you're not to come back till you have. I mean it.'

'I don't suppose for a moment - '

'Rubbish! A woman knows. She went home and cried; I know she did, and she's counting the minutes till you see her again. Now, I've lots to do, and you're frightfully in the way. Good-bye.' She held out her hand.

He rose.

'You send me away definitely?'

'Definitely. Your liking for me is pure perverseness.'

'It's pure adoration,' said Cecil.

'I don't think so. It's imagination. However, whatever it is I don't want it.'

'Good-bye, then,' said Cecil.

He went to the door.

'You can let me know when you've seen her.'

'I don't suppose she'll see me.'

'Yes, she will now. It's the psychological moment.'

'You shan't be bothered with me any more, anyhow,' said Cecil in a low voice.

'Good. And do what I tell you.'

He shut the shabby door of the little house with a loud bang, and went out with a great longing to do something vaguely desperate.

Lunch produced a different mood. He said to himself that he wouldn't think of Mrs Raymond any more, and went to call on Hyacinth.

The servant told him she was out.

He was just turning away when Anne Yeo came out. She glanced at him with malicious satisfaction.

'Hyacinth's gone to the National Gallery,' she volunteered. 'Did you want to see her? You will find her there.'

Cecil walked a few steps with her.

'I'm going to the greengrocer's,' continued Anne, 'to complain.' She held a little book in her hand, and he noticed that she wore a golf cap, thick boots, and a mackintosh, although it was a beautiful day.

'I always dress like this,' she said, 'when I'm going to complain of prices. Isn't it a glorious day? The sort of day when everyone feels happy and hopeful.'

'I don't feel either,' said Cecil candidly.

'No, you don't look it. Why not go and see some pictures?'

He smiled. They parted at the corner.

Then Cecil, without leaving any message for Hyacinth, jumped into a hansom, giving the man the address of his club in Pall Mall. On the way he changed his mind, and drove to the National Gallery. As he went up the steps his spirits rose. He thought he recognised Miss Verney's motor waiting outside. There was something of an adventure in following her here. He would pretend it was an accident, and not let her know yet that he had called.

He wandered through the rooms, which were very empty, and came upon Hyacinth seated on a red velvet seat opposite a Botticelli.

She looked more dejected than he could have thought possible, her type being specially formed to express the joy of life. It was impossible to help feeling a thrill of flattered vanity when he saw the sudden change in her expression and her deep blush when she recognised him.

'I didn't know you ever came here,' she said, as they shook hands.

'It's a curious coincidence I should meet you when, for once in my life, I come to study the Primitives,' said Cecil.

He then seated himself beside her.

'Don't you think all that' – he waved his hand towards the pictures – 'is rather a superstition?'

'Perhaps; but it's glorious, I think. These are the only pictures that give me perfect satisfaction. All others, however good they are, have the effect of making me restless,' said Hyacinth.

'I haven't had a moment's rest,' said Cecil, 'since I saw you yesterday afternoon. Why were you so unkind?'

'Was it unkind?' she asked. Her face was illuminated.

They spent an hour together; had horrible tea in the dismal refreshment-room, and having agreed that it seemed a shame to spend a lovely day within these walls, he said –

'I don't think I've ever met you out of doors – in the open air, I mean.'

'It would be nice,' said Hyacinth.

He proposed that they should do something unconventional and delightful, and meet the next day in Kensington

Gardens, which he assured her was just as good as the country just now. She agreed, and they made an appointment.

'How is Mrs Raymond?' she then asked abruptly.

'I don't know. Mrs Raymond – she's charming, and a great friend of mine, of course; but we've quarrelled. At least I'm not going to see her again.'

'Poor Mrs Raymond!' exclaimed Hyacinth. 'Or perhaps I ought to be sorry for you?'

'No, not if you let me see you sometimes.' He looked at her radiant face and felt the soothing, rather intoxicating, effect of her admiration after Eugenia's coldness. . . . He took her hand and held it for a minute, and then they parted with the prospect of meeting the next day.

Hyacinth went home too happy even to speak to Anne about it. She was filled with hope. He *must* care for her.

And Cecil felt as if he were a strange, newly-invented kind of criminal. Either, he said to himself, he was playing with the feelings of this dear, beautiful creature, or he was drifting into a *mariage de convenance*, a vulgar and mercenary speculation, while all the time he was madly devoted to someone else. He felt guilty, anxious, and furious with Eugenia. But she had really meant what she said that morning; she wouldn't see him again. But the thought of seeing Hyacinth under the trees the next morning – a secret appointment, too! – was certainly consoling.

With a sudden sensation of being utterly sick of himself and his feelings, tired of both Hyacinth and Eugenia, and bored to death at the idea of all women, Cecil went to see Lord Selsey.

More of the little Ottleys

'FANCY!' said Edith.

'Fancy what?'

'Somehow I never should have thought it,' said Edith thoughtfully.

'Never should have thought what? You have a way of assuming. I know the end of your story before I've heard the beginning. It's an annoying method,' said Bruce.

'I shouldn't have been so surprised if they had been anywhere else. But just *there*,' continued Edith.

'Who? and where?'

'Perhaps I'd better not tell you,' Edith said.

They had just finished dinner, and she got up as if to ring the bell for coffee.

He stopped her.

'No! Don't ring; I don't wish Bennett to be present at a painful scene.'

Edith looked at him. 'I didn't know there was going to be a painful scene. What's the matter?'

'Naturally, I'm distressed and hurt at your conduct.'

'Conduct!'

'Don't echo my words, Edith.'

She saw he looked really distressed.

'Naturally,' he continued, 'I'm hurt at your keeping things from me. Your own husband! I may have my faults – '

She nodded.

'But I've not deserved this from you.'

'Oh dear, Bruce, I was only thinking. I'm sorry if I was irritating. I will tell you.'

'Go on.'

'When Nurse and Archie were out in the Gardens this morning, *who* do you think they met?'

'This is not a game. I'm not going to guess. You seem to take me for a child.'

'Well, you won't tell anybody, will you?'

'That depends. I'm not going to make any promises beforehand. I shall act on my own judgement.'

'Oh you might promise. Well, I'll trust you.'

'Thanks! I should think so!'

'They met Hyacinth, walking with Cecil Reeve alone in a quiet part of the Gardens. They weren't walking.'

'Then why did you say they were?' asked Bruce severely.

'It's the same thing. They were sitting down.'

'How *can* it be the same thing?'

'Oh, don't worry, Bruce! They were sitting down under a tree and Nurse saw them holding hands.'

Bruce looked horrified.

'Holding hands,' continued Edith; 'and I can't help thinking they must be engaged. Isn't it extraordinary Hyacinth hasn't told me? What do you think?'

Bruce got up from the table, lighted a cigarette, and walked round the little room.

'I don't know. I must consider. I must think it over.' He paused a minute. 'I am pained. Pained and surprised. A girl like Hyacinth, a friend of yours, behaving like a housemaid out with a soldier in the open street!'

'It wasn't the street, Bruce.'

'It's the same idea.'

'Quite a quiet part of the Gardens.'

'That makes their conduct worse. I scarcely think, after what you have told me, that I can allow you to go out with Hyacinth tomorrow.'

'How can you be so absurd? I must go; I want to hear about it.'

'Have I ever made any objection till now at your great intimacy with Hyacinth Verney? Of course not. Because I was deceived in her.'

'Deceived?'

'Don't repeat my words, Edith. I won't have it! Certainly I was deceived. I thought she was a fitting companion for you – I *thought* so.'

'Oh, Bruce, really! Where's the harm? Perhaps they're engaged; and if they are I think it is charming. Cecil is such a nice, amusing good-looking boy, and – '

'I formed my opinion of Reeve some time ago.'

'You only met him once.'

'Once is more than enough for me to form a judgement of anyone. He is absolutely unworthy of her. But *her* conduct I regard as infinitely worse. I always imagined she was respectably brought up – a lady!'

'Good gracious! Anyone can see *that*! She's the most charming girl in the world.'

'*Outwardly*, no doubt, she *seems* all right. But now you see what she is.'

He paused to relight his cigarette, which had gone out, and continued: 'Such behaviour would be dreadful enough in private, but in public! Do you think of the example?'

'The example to Archie, do you mean?'

'Don't laugh, Edith. This is no matter for laughing. Certainly to Archie – to anyone. Now I've only one thing to say.'

'Do say it.'

'That I never wish to hear Hyacinth Verney's name mentioned again. You are never to speak of her to me. Do you hear?'

'Yes, Bruce.'

'It is such a disillusion. I'm so shocked, so horrified, finding her a snake in the grass.'

'Oh, I'm sure she didn't look a bit like a snake, Bruce. She wore that lovely grey dress and a hat with roses.'

'How do you know? Did *Archie* tell you? No; you lowered yourself to question Nurse. A nice opinion Nurse must have of your friends now! No; *that's* over. I won't blame *you*, dear, but I must never hear anything more about Hyacinth.'

Edith sat down and took up a book.

'Why is there no coffee?' asked Bruce rather loudly.

'Oh, you said I wasn't to ring.'

She rang.

While the parlourmaid was bringing in the coffee, Bruce said in a high, condescending voice –

'Have you seen that interesting article in the evening paper, dear, about the Solicitor-General?'

'Which do you mean? "Silk and Stuff"?'

'Yes. Read it – read it and improve your mind. Far better for a woman to occupy her mind with general subjects, and make herself intellectually a companion for her husband – are you listening? – than to be always gossiping and thinking about people and their paltry private affairs. Do you hear?'

'Yes, dear.'

He took his coffee and then said –

'In what direction did you say they were going?'

'Oh, I thought you didn't want me to speak of her again. They were going in the opposite direction.'

'Opposite to what? Now that's the curious difference between a woman's intellect and a man's. You can't be logical! What do you mean by "opposite"?'

'Why, Bruce, I mean just opposite. The other way.'

'Do you mean they walked off separately?'

'Oh, *no*! They were going away together, and looking so happy. But really, Bruce, I'm sorry I bothered you, telling you about it. I had no idea you would feel it so much.'

'What do you mean? Feel it? Of course, I'm terribly distressed to find that a wife of mine is intimate with such people – where are you going?'

'I was going to write to Hyacinth and tell her I can't go out with her tomorrow.'

'Why can't you go out with her?'

'You said I was never to see her again.'

'Yes; but don't be in a hurry. Never be impulsive.' He waited a minute; she stood by the door. 'On the whole, since you wish it so much, I will permit you to go out with her this once – for the last time, of course – so that you can find out if she really is engaged to be married to that young ass. What a mercenary scoundrel he must be!'

'I don't think that. Anyone would admire her, and he is very well-off himself.'

'Well-off! Do you consider that to his credit? So should I be well-off I had relations that died and left me a lot of money. Don't defend him, Edith; his conduct is simply disgraceful. What right has he to expect to marry a beautiful girl in Hyacinth's position? Good gracious, does he want everything?'

'I suppose – he likes her.'

'That's not particularly clever of him. So would any man. What I object to so much about that empty-headed cad, is that he's never satisfied. He wants the earth, it seems to me!'

'Really, Bruce, one would think you were quite – '

'What?'

'Well, quite jealous of him, to hear you talk. If one didn't know that – of course you can't be,' she added quickly.

'This incident is now closed,' said Bruce. 'We will never discuss the subject again.'

'Very well, dear.'

She then went into the little drawing-room and looked longingly at the telephone. She feared there would be no chance of communicating with her friend that evening.

Five minutes later Bruce came in and said –

'And what can old Cannon be about to allow his ward to be tearing about all over London with a man of Reeve's antecedents?'

'What's the matter wih his antecedents? I didn't know he had any.'

'Don't interrupt. And Miss Yeo? Where was Miss Yeo, I should like to know?'

'I can't *think*.'

'A nice way she does her duty as chaperone!'

'Dear, Hyacinth's twenty-three, not a child. Miss Yeo's her companion; but she can't insist, even if she wants to, on following Hyacinth about if she doesn't wish it.'

'She should wish it. Seriously, do you think Sir Charles knows of these goings-on – I mean of this conduct?'

'I shouldn't think he knew the details.'

'Then isn't it my duty as a married man and father of a family – '

Edith concealed a smile by moving the screen.

'To communicate with him on the subject?'

Edith had a moment's terror. It struck her that if she opposed him, Bruce was capable of doing it. He often wrote letters beginning, 'Sir, I feel it my duty,' to people on subjects that were no earthly concern of his. If he really did anything of this sort, Hyacinth would never forgive her.

After a second's concentration of mind, she said mildly –

'Perhaps you had better, if you really feel it your duty. Of course, I'd rather you didn't, personally. But if that's how you feel about it – '

Bruce wheeled round at once.

'Indeed! Well, I shall not do anything of the sort. Is it my business to open her guardian's eyes? Why should I? No; I won't interfere in the matter at all. Let them go their own way. Do you hear, Edith? Let them do just whatever they like.'

'Yes; I was going to.'

'Mind you, they'll be wretched,' he added rather vindictively. 'If I only saw a chance of happiness for them I shouldn't mind so much.'

'Why, do you think they will be miserable if they are married?'

'Of course they will. People who behave in that unprincipled way before – '

'Why, we used to sit in the garden,' said Edith timidly.

'Oh, yes, of course; after your father had given his consent.'

'And once or twice before.'

Bruce smiled rather fatuously. 'Don't compare the two cases. I was a man of the world. . . . I was very firm, wasn't I, Edith? Somehow at first your father didn't seem to like me, but I reasoned with him. I always reason calmly with people. And then he came round. Do you remember how pleased you were that day?' He patted Edith's hair.

'Then why be so severe?'

'Perhaps I am a little bit too severe,' he acknowledged. 'But you don't quite understand how it jars on me to think of any friend of yours behaving in a manner that's – are you sure they're engaged?'

'No; I don't know anything about it.'

'Well, of course, if they don't marry after what Archie has seen, it will be a public scandal, that's all I can say. On the other hand, of course, it would be far better not.'

'What do you propose?' said Edith.

'I don't quite know; I'll think it over. Look here, Edith, if you don't mind, I think I'll go for a little stroll. The flat seems so hot and airless tonight.'

Edith glanced at the telephone.

'Oh, don't go,' she said.

He went into the hall and put on his coat. 'I must go, dear. I feel the need of air. I shan't be long.'

'You will only go for a little walk, won't you?'

'I *might* go to the club for half an hour. I shall see. Good night, dear.'

'Good night.'

He came back to say, in a rather mysterious voice –

'What were Nurse's exact words?'

CHAPTER THIRTEEN

'Oh, she said, "Miss Verney seemed to be carrying on anyhow with a young gentleman in Kensington Gardens," and then she said it was Mr Reeve, that's all.'

'Disgusting! Horrible!'

He went out and banged the door.

Edith went to the telephone.

Lady Cannon's visit

LADY CANNON got up one morning earlier than usual and tried on a dress of last season, which she found was a little too tight. For this, naturally, she blamed her maid with some severity. She then dressed rather hurriedly and went all over the house, touching little ornaments with the tip of her finger, saying that the pictures in the drawing-room were crooked, and that nothing had been properly dusted. Having sent for the housemaid and scolded her, and given the second footman notice, she felt better, but was still sufficiently in what is expressively called a bad temper to feel an inclination to do disagreeable duties, so she made up her mind to call and see her husband's ward, and tell her something she would not like to hear. For Hyacinth she always felt a curious mixture of chronic anger, family pride, and admiring disapproval, which combination she had never yet discovered to be a common form of vague jealousy.

Lady Cannon arrived about three o'clock, pompously dressed in tight purple velvet and furs. She thought she saw two heads appear at the studio window and then vanish, but was told that Miss Verney was out.

CHAPTER FOURTEEN

Prompted by a determination not to be baffled, she said she would get out and write a note, and was shown to the drawing-room.

Anne, in a peculiarly hideous and unnecessary apron of black alpaca, came in, bringing a little writing-case.

'Oh! Miss Yeo, as you're there, I needn't write the letter. You can give Hyacinth a message for me.'

'Certainly, Lady Cannon.'

'How is it that she is out at this extraordinary hour?'

'Is there anything extraordinary about the hour?' asked Anne, looking at the clock. 'It's three; somehow I always regard three as a particularly ordinary hour.'

'I differ from you, Miss Yeo.'

'Anyhow, it happens every day,' murmured Anne.

'Was Hyacinth out to lunch?' said Lady Cannon.

'No - no. She lunched at home.'

'Do you think she'll be long?'

'Oh, no; I shouldn't think she would be many minutes.'

'Then I think I'll wait.'

'*Do*,' said Anne cordially.

'I wanted to speak to her. Considering she's my husband's ward, I see very, very little of Hyacinth, Miss Yeo.'

'Yes, she was saying the other day that you hardly ever called now,' Anne said conciliatingly.

'Has she been quite well lately?'

'Oh, do you know, she's been *so* well,' said Anne, in a high, affected voice, which she knew was intensely irritating. 'So very, very well!'

Anne then stood up.

'Would you like a cup of tea, or coffee, while you're waiting?'

'*Tea?* At three o'clock in the afternoon! I never heard of such a thing. You seem to have strangely Bohemian ideas in this house, Miss Yeo!'

'Do you think tea Bohemian? Well, coffee then?'

Lady Cannon hesitated, but wishing for an excuse to wait, she said –

'Thank you, if it isn't giving any trouble; perhaps I'll take a cup of coffee. I didn't have any after lunch.'

'Oh, yes, do. I'll go and order it at once.'

Anne walked with slow, languid dignity to the door, and when she had shut it, flew like a hunted hare to the studio, where Cecil Reeve and Hyacinth were sitting together.

'Hyacinth,' she said sharply, 'run upstairs at once, put on your hat, go to the hall door and bang it, and come into the drawing-room. Lady Cannon's going to stop the whole afternoon. She's in an appalling temper.'

'She won't wait long,' exclaimed Hyacinth, 'surely?'

'Won't she? She's ordered coffee. She'll be smoking a cigarette before you know where you are.'

'Oh, I'll go,' said Cecil. 'Let me go.'

'Of course you must go,' said Anne. 'You can come back in an hour.'

'But, good heavens, Anne,' said Hyacinth, 'why on earth should we make a secret of Mr Reeve being here?'

'Why, because I said you were out.'

'Well, I'll go and explain,' said Hyacinth.

'Indeed you won't. You're not to go and give me away. Besides, I won't be baffled by that old cat. She's suspicious already. Out you go!'

Cecil took his hat and stick, and went out of the front door.

Anne ran upstairs, brought down Hyacinth's hat, veil, and gloves, and pushed her towards the drawing-room.

'Don't you see? – she'll think you've just come in,' said Anne.

'What about the coachman and footman?'

Oh, good heavens, *do* you think they're going to call on her and tell her all about it?'

Just as Hyacinth, laughing, was going into the drawing-room, Anne clutched her, and said –

'I don't know that you'd better be at home after all! Charles will be calling directly. Oh, I forgot, he won't come in when he sees the carriage.'

Anne relaxed her clasp and went to order coffee.

Lady Cannon was looking angrily in the glass when Hyacinth came in.

'Oh, here you are, my dear. I'm glad I didn't miss you. I wanted to speak to you about something.'

'Yes, Auntie.'

Lady Cannon coughed, and said rather portentously, 'You must not be offended with me, dear. You know, in a sense I'm, as it were, in the place of your mother – or, at any rate, your stepmother.'

'Yes.'

'Of course you're perfectly free to do exactly as you like, but I heard in a roundabout way something that rather surprised me about you.'

'What is it?'

'We were dining with some friends last night' (it was characteristic of Lady Cannon not to mention their names), 'where we happened to meet that young couple, the Ottleys. You know Mrs Ottley very well, I believe?'

'Edith is my greatest friend,' said Hyacinth.

'Quite so; she seems a very nice young woman. Very devoted to her husband. And I think him a most superior man! He sat next to me at dinner, and I had quite a long talk with him. We spoke of you. He told me something that surprised me so much. He said that you had been seen very frequently lately about alone with a young man. Is this a fact?'

'What did he say about it?'

'Well, he seemed to regret it – he seemed to think it was a pity. Living alone as you do, it certainly is not the right thing for you to be seen anywhere without Miss Yeo.'

Hyacinth became crimson. 'On what grounds did Mr Ottley find fault with anything I do?'

'Merely general grounds, my dear. A very proper dislike to the flighty behaviour of the girls of the present day. As he tells me, he feels it as a father – '

'Father! He has only a little boy of two. I think it's very impertinent of him to talk of me like that at all.'

'On the contrary, I thought it exceedingly nice of him. He sincerely wishes you well, Hyacinth. Oh, *how* well that young man wishes you! Make no mistake about it. By the way, I promised him not to mention his name in the matter. So of course you won't repeat it. But I was really rather upset at what he said. I haven't said anything to Sir Charles yet, as I thought you might give me some explanation.'

'I have no explanation to give. I suppose you know who it is I was walking with?'

'I gathered that it was a Mr Reeve. Now, Hyacinth dear, you know how much I wish you well; if you're engaged, I think your guardian and I ought to know it, and in any case you should be more discreet in your behaviour.'

Hyacinth's eyes flashed.

'Are you engaged?' asked Lady Cannon.

'I must decline to answer. I recognise no right that you or anyone else has to ask me such a question.'

Lady Cannon rose indignantly, leaving her coffee untouched.

'Very well, Hyacinth; if this is the way you take my kind advice and well-meant interest, there's nothing more to be said. Of course, I shall tell Sir Charles what I've heard. From what I can gather from that excellent young man Mr Ottley, Mr Reeve is by no means a person that Sir Charles and I would be glad to welcome with open arms, as one of the family.'

'Cecil Reeve is a friend of mine. There's nothing in the world to be said against him, and you must really allow me the privilege of choosing my own friends.'

'Good-bye then,' said Lady Cannon, going to the door. 'I'm pained, grieved, and shocked at your attitude. I can only presume, however, that you are not engaged to be married, for surely your first thought would have been to ask your guardian's consent; and once more let me tell you, in being reckless as you have, you're simply ruining your future.'

With this Lady Cannon swept from the room.

She returned, however, and said, 'I regard all this as not your own fault, Hyacinth, but the fault of *that Miss Yeo*. From the first I saw she had an evil influence, and I've been proved, as, perhaps unfortunately, I always am, to be perfectly right.'

'The worst of it was,' Hyacinth said, when relating the conversation to Anne a little later, 'that I *can't* tell Auntie that I'm engaged. Isn't it awful?'

'You soon will be,' said Anne consolingly.

'Do you really think so?'

'Yes, and I'm glad Lady Cannon was scored off, anyhow.'

'Edith told me about her having mentioned to Bruce about our meeting the nurse and baby. She was very sorry, but I thought it didn't matter a bit. Why do you think Bruce tried to make mischief in this horrid way?'

'Only because he's a fool. Like so many of us, he's in love with you,' said Anne.

Hyacinth laughed, thinking Anne was in fun.

Raggett in Love

'IF you please, ma'am, a gentleman called and left some flowers.'

'Who was it?' said Edith.

'He wouldn't give his name. There's a note for you.'

Edith went into the drawing-room, where she found a large bundle of lilies, violets, and daffodils, and the following letter, written in a cramped, untidy handwriting –

DEAR MRS OTTLEY,

I went for a bicycle ride yesterday and plucked these -flowers for you, hoping you wouldn't mind accepting them. If you have a moment's time to give me, I wonder if you would let me call and see you one day?

Sincerely yours,

F. J. RAGGETT

P.S. – I'm extremely busy, but am free at any time. Perhaps tomorrow might suit you? Or if you're engaged tomorrow, perhaps today? I would ask you to ring me up and kindly let me know, but I'm not on the telephone.

CHAPTER FIFTEEN

Edith was amused, but also a little bored. Ever since the dinner at the Savoy, now a fortnight ago, Raggett had been showing furtive signs of a wild admiration for her, at the same time hedging absurdly by asking her to tell him when he might call and giving no address, and by (for instance) pretending he had plucked the flowers himself, evidently not knowing that they had been sent with her address written on a card printed with the name of Cooper's Stores in the Edgware Road.

She never knew how Bruce would take things, so she had not said anything about it to him yet. He seemed to have forgotten the existence of Raggett, and never mentioned him now.

She arranged the flowers in some blue and white china vases, and sat down by the window in the little drawing-room. She had before her, until Bruce would come home to dinner, two of those empty hours which all young married women in her position have known. There was nothing to do. Archie was still out, and she was tired of reading, and disliked needlework.

She had just come back from seeing Hyacinth. How full and interesting *her* life seemed! At any rate, *she* had everything before her. Edith felt as if she herself were locked up in a box. Even her endless patience with Bruce was beginning to pall a little.

As she was thinking these things she heard a ring, and the maid came in and said –

'It's the gentleman that left the flowers, and could you see him in a minute?'

'Certainly.'

Raggett came in. He looked just as extraordinary as he had at the Savoy and as difficult to place. His manner could not be said to express anything, for he had no manner, but his voice was the voice of a shy undergraduate, while his clothes, Edith thought, suggested a combination of a bushranger and a conjuror. His tie, evidently new, was a marvel, a sort of true-lover's knot of red patterned with green, strange beyond description. He seemed terrified.

'How very kind of you to come and see me,' she said in her sweetest voice, 'and these lovely flowers! They quite brighten one up.'

'I'm glad you think they're all right,' said Raggett in a low voice.

'They're beautiful. Fancy your plucking them all yourself! Where did you find these lovely lilies growing? I always fancied they were hot-house plants.'

'Oh, I was bicycling,' Raggett said. 'I just saw them, you know. I thought you might like them. How is Ottley?'

'Bruce is very well. Haven't you seen him lately?'

'Not very. I've been working so fearfully hard,' he said; 'at the British Museum chiefly. One doesn't run up against Bruce there much.'

'No. I suppose he hardly ever goes.'

There was a pause.

'Won't you have some tea?' asked Edith.

'No, thank you. I never take it.'

And there was another silence.

Just as Edith was rather at a loss, and was beginning a sentence with –

'Have you been – ' he at the same time said –

'Do you know – ?'

'I beg your pardon,' said Edith.

'Oh, I beg yours.'

'Do say what you were going to say.'

'Oh, please finish your sentence.'

'I wasn't going to say anything.'

'Nor was I.'

'I was going to ask you if you'd been to the Savoy again lately?'

'No; I've only been there once in my life. It was a great event for me, Mrs Ottley.'

'Really?'

He spoke with more confidence, but in a still lower voice.

'Yes. I met my ideal there.'

He fixed on her an ardent but respectful glare.

She smiled.

'I'm afraid,' continued Raggett, 'that I'm not amusing you much. I suppose you're very fond of wit and gaiety? I wasn't brought up in a very humorous atmosphere. I don't think I ever heard a joke till quite recently.'

Edith laughed.

'My father,' he went on, 'used sometimes to say at night, "Now it's time for Bedfordshire," but I wasn't amused at that after ten years old. My family are really very serious as a whole. I should never dream of asking them even a riddle, because I'm sure they would give it up at once.'

'Did you say you heard one joke recently? What was it?' asked Edith.

Raggett blushed and looked down.

'I'm very sorry, but I'm afraid I can't tell you, Mrs Ottley. Not that I forget it, but it isn't suited to your – well, to your atmosphere' – he looked round the room.

'Oh! Can't you *arrange* it?'

'Impossible,' he said firmly. 'Quite impossible.'

'Oh well, of course – '

'Impossible,' he repeated, shaking his head.

'Do you go much to the theatre?' she asked conversationally.

'Never. It would interfere with my work.'

'What is your work, exactly?' she asked, with polite interest.

'It's difficult to explain, Mrs Ottley. It takes a great many forms.'

'Oh, yes.'

'Just at this moment I'm a Legitimist – you understand, don't you? We drink to Queen Mary over the water – and put violets on the statue of King Charles the Martyr in February, and so forth.'

'Ah. That must be very hard work.'

'Oh, it isn't only that – I'm a kind of Secretary, you see, to the Society.'

'Really? Really? What fun it must be; I mean how interesting. Can I belong?'

'Oh, dear yes, of course, Mrs Ottley. If you liked.'

'What should I have to do?'

'Well, first of all you would have to pay a shilling.'

'Yes?'

'And then you would be eligible for a year's probation.'

'And what should we do after that?'

'Well, after that, you see, we shall have to bide our time.'

'That doesn't sound very hard,' said Edith thoughtfully. 'Just to pay a shilling and bide your time.'

'I'll send you some papers about it, if you really take any interest.'

'Thanks. Thanks, very much. Yes, do send them.'

'Do you really think you would care to become a member, Mrs Ottley?'

'Oh, yes; yes, I should think so. I always hated Oliver Cromwell.'

He looked doubtful.

'Yes, of course – but that alone, I'm afraid, would hardly be . . . you see there might be a revolution at any moment.'

'I see. But – excuse my asking you, what has that to do with the British Museum?'

'I can hardly tell you off-hand like this, Mrs Ottley; but if you let me come again one day – '

'Oh, certainly, do – do come again.'

'Then I'll say good-bye for today,' said Raggett, with an admiring look. 'I – I hope I haven't trespassed on your valuable – '

'Oh, no; not in the least.'

'I've enjoyed our talk so much,' said Raggett, lingering.

'So have I, Mr Raggett. It has been most interesting.'

'I – I felt,' said Raggett, now standing up and looking very shy, 'I somehow felt at once that there was a kind of – may I say, sympathy?'

'Quite so.'

'Yes? Well, give my kind regards to Ottley, and thank you so much.'

They shook hands, she rang the bell, and he rushed out as if he was in a violent hurry, leaving Edith rather bewildered.

At dinner that evening Edith said –

'Fancy, Bruce, Raggett called today!'

Bruce dropped his spoon in the soup and looked up.

'*Raggett?* He – do you mean to say he came here?'

'Yes. He paid a visit. Why shouldn't he?'

'I don't know, but it seems a very odd thing. He never pays visits. What did he seem to think of the flat?'

'He didn't say. He talked about his work.'

'What did you think of him?' asked Bruce.

'He seemed very vague. He's very good-natured; fancy his sending me all those flowers!'

'He sent you flowers?' said Bruce slowly. '*Raggett!*'

'Surely you don't mind?'

Bruce waited a minute and said, 'We'll talk it over after dinner.'

There was an uneasy pause; then Edith said –

'I saw Hyacinth today. She had just had a visit from Lady Cannon.'

Bruce looked rather guilty and uncomfortable.

'I like Lady Cannon,' he said presently. 'She's a woman of sound sense. She has a very strong feeling of responsibility about Hyacinth.'

'Yes.' Edith and Hyacinth had arranged not to say any more, as it would be useless.

'A very discreet woman, too,' continued Bruce. 'And what news about Hyacinth?'

'None, I think. She seems very happy.'

'Happy! *That* can't last.'

After dinner Bruce followed Edith into the drawing-room, looked angrily at the flowers and said –

'Now, what's the meaning of all this? Mind, I'm not jealous. It isn't my nature to be. What I dislike is being made a fool of. If I thought that Raggett, after all I've done for him – '

'Oh, Bruce! How can you be so absurd? A poor harmless creature – '

'Harmless creature, indeed! I think it extremely marked, calling on you when I was out.'

'He didn't know you were out. It's the usual time to pay a visit, and he really came just to ask me to belong to the Society.'

'I don't call Raggett a society man.'

'He's a secret-society man,' said Edith. 'He wants me to be a Legitimist.'

'Now I won't have any nonsense of that sort here,' said Bruce, striking the table with his fist. 'Goodness knows where it will end. That sort of thing takes women away from the natural home duties, and I disapprove of it strongly. Why, he'll soon be asking you to be a Suffragette! I think I shall write to Raggett.'

'Oh, would you, really?'

'I shall write to him,' repeated Bruce, 'and tell him that I won't have these constant visits and marked attentions. I shall say you complained to me. Yes, that's the dignified way, and I shall request him to keep his secret societies to himself, and not to try to interfere with the peace and harmony of a happy English home.'

He drew some writing-paper towards him.

'I'm sure he didn't mean the slightest harm. He thought it was the proper thing, after dining with us.'

'But it isn't like the man, Edith! It isn't Raggett! He's no slave to convention; don't think it. I can't help fancying that there must have been some ulterior motive. It seems to me sinister – that's the word – sinister.'

'Would you think it sinister if he never came again?'

'Well, perhaps not, but in allowing this to pass – isn't it the thin end of the wedge?'

'Give him a chance and see,' she said. 'Don't be in a hurry. After all, he's your great friend. You're always talking to me about him; and what's he done? – sent a few flowers and called here once. I'm sure he thought you would like it.'

'But don't you see, Edith, the attention should have been paid to me, not to you.'

'He could hardly send you flowers, Bruce. I'm sure he thought it was the proper thing.'

Bruce walked up and down the room greatly agitated.

'I admit that this is a matter that requires consideration. I shouldn't like to make a mountain out of a mole-hill. We'll see; we'll give him a chance. But if he comes here again, or takes any step to persuade you to have anything to do with his Society or whatever it is, I shall know how to act.'

'Of course you will, dear.'

Edith hoped she wouldn't receive a large envelope full of papers about the Legitimists by the first post.

'I hope you know, Bruce, I shouldn't care if I never saw him again.'

'Why not? Because he's my friend, I suppose? You look down on him just because he's a hard worker, and of some use in the world – not a dandified, conventional, wasp-waisted idiot like Cecil Reeve! Perhaps you prefer Cecil Reeve?'

'Much,' replied Edith firmly.

'Why? Let's hear your reasons.'

'Why, he's a real person. I know where I am when I'm talking to him – we're on the same platform.'

'Platform?'

'Yes. When I talk to Mr Raggett I feel as if he had arrived at Victoria, and I had gone to meet him at Charing Cross. Do you see? We don't get near enough to understand each other.'

'Quite near enough,' replied Bruce suspiciously. Then he said, 'I feel the want of air. If you don't mind, dear, I think I shall go for a stroll.'

'Oh, don't!'

He went to the hall and put on his coat.

'Just a stroll; or I may look in at the club. You don't understand; a man feels rather cramped in these surroundings, Edith.'

CHAPTER FIFTEEN

'I quite understand your feeling.'

'I shan't be long,' said Bruce. 'Try and make up your mind to give up Raggett's society altogether. You don't mind making this sacrifice for me, do you?'

'Not in the least,' she answered. 'I prefer it.'

He went out.

Archie

IT was Sunday afternoon, and Bruce, lunch still pervading his consciousness, found himself reading over and over again and taking a kind of stupefied interest in the 'Answers to Correspondents' in a certain Sunday paper, and marvelling at the mine of extraordinary miscellaneous information possessed by the person who answered them.

'Brief replies: –

'To *Miserable Alfred* (Baldness). – If you comply with the rules, will send private advice.

'*Knutford* (For knee trouble). – My advice is against.' (Bruce vaguely thought this rather harsh. If Knutford liked knee trouble why shouldn't he have it?)

'*Alter Ego* (Tomato culture). – There's no need to soak the seeds for days. The man who sows in wet soil and then treads down flat foredooms himself to complete failure. This is, however, nothing to go by. If seed be purchased let it be from a trustworthy firm. Personally, I think in the case of outdoor tomatoes the middle course is best.

'*Worried* (Photography). – To avoid curling. The chief trouble with reel films is their tendency to curl. In any case the film should be allowed to soak for five minutes, and I need not dwell upon other methods of treating the latter kind. All my remarks on plate development, etc., apply equally to cut films, as I should almost have thought "Worried" would have gathered by now.

'*True Blue* (Egg-preserving). – We quite understand your desire to make more headway than you can in a south-coast watering-place . . .'

At this moment Edith came in. Bruce looked up, a little annoyed at the interruption. He was becoming quite absorbed in the egg-preserving case on the south coast, and morbidly anxious to know what would happen next.

'Bruce, I wonder if you'd do me a very great favour? It really isn't difficult. I've allowed Nurse to go out and Bennett is busy, and I wanted to fly over just for a minute or two to see Hyacinth. She telephoned to me. I shouldn't be gone more than twenty minutes.'

'Of course, go. Do go. I don't want you. I'm very busy.'

He took up the paper again.

'It isn't that; but *would* you very much mind looking after Archie while I'm gone? He'll be perfectly good. I'll give him his box of toys, and he'll sit in the corner over there and you'll never notice he's there till I'm back again.'

'Of course, of course. Surely I'm capable of looking after my own son. Do go.'

'Yes, Bruce dear. And if he asks for anything just nod and smile and don't give it to him, and he'll be all right.'

'Oh, don't worry.'

As she was going out he called out –

'And I say, Edith, just give him a hint that I've got some rather important work to do, and he mustn't interrupt me by asking foolish questions.'

'Yes, oh yes. I'm so glad to think you're so sensible, and not ridiculously nervous of having to look after the child.'

'Nervous? What rot! I never heard such nonsense. I say, Edith, what's the doctor's address? In case he has a fit, or anything.'

'Oh, Bruce! As if he would *dream* of having a fit! I shan't give you the address. You'd be telephoning to him on the chance. Good gracious, don't make such a fuss! I shall only be gone a few minutes.'

'I'm not making a fuss. It's you. Fancy thinking it necessary to tell me not to give him what he asks for! As if I should.'

He returned to his paper, and Edith brought in the little boy.

He gave his father a keen glance from under his smooth, fair fringe and sat down in front of the box of toys.

As soon as Edith had gone he held out a card to his father, and said –

'E for efalunt.'

Bruce frowned, nodded, waved his hand, and went on reading.

He had lost the thread of the Egg Question, but became equally absorbed in the following problem.

'*Disheartened.* – You must make a quiet but determined stand against such imposition. It does not follow because you walked out with a young man two or three times, and he now walks out with your friend instead, that . . . '

'X for swordfish,' said Archie, holding out another card.

'Don't talk, Archie.'

'I've got my best suit on,' said Archie.

'Yes.'

'What I was photographed in.'

'Don't talk, old chap. I want to read.'

'This is my bear. It's the same bear.'

'The same bear as what?'

'Why, the same bear! This is a soldier.'

He put the wooden soldier in his mouth, then put it carefully back in the box.

'This is my bear,' said Archie again. 'Just the same bear. That's all.'

Bruce threw away the paper.

'You want to have a talk, eh?' he said.

'This is my best suit,' said Archie. 'Have you any sugar in your pockets?'

'Sugar in my pockets? Who put that into your head?'

'Nobody didn't put it in my head. Don't you put any in your pocket?'

'No. Sugar, indeed! I'm not a parrot.'

Archie roared with laughter.

'You're not a parrot!' he said, laughing loudly. 'Wouldn't it be fun if you was a parrot. I wish you was a parrot.'

'Don't be foolish, Archie.'

'Do parrots keep sugar in their pockets?'

'Don't be silly.'

'Have parrots got pockets?'

'Play with your soldiers, dear.'

'Do parrots have pockets?'

'Don't be a nuisance.'

'Why did you say parrots had sugar in their pockets, then?'

'I never said anything of the kind.'

'What do parrots have pockets for?'

'Do you think your mother will be long?'

'Will mother know about parrots and pockets?'

'You're talking nonsense, Archie. Now be good. Your mother said you would be good.'

'Is it naughty to talk about parrots – with pockets?'

'Yes.'

'Then you're very naughty. You talk about them.'

'Will you stop talking about them if I get you some sugar?' said Bruce, feeling frightfully ashamed of himself, but fearing for his reason if Archie said any more on the subject.

'I'm a good boy. I'll stop talking about parrots if you get me some sugar.'

He put his hand in his father's with a most winning smile.

'I'll show you where it is. It's in the kitchen. It's in the nursery, too, but it's nicer sugar in the kitchen.'

'I oughtn't to give it you. Your mother will be angry.'

'Do parrots have pockets?'

Bruce jumped up and went with the child, and told the cook to give him six lumps of sugar.

She seemed surprised, amused, and doubtful.

'Do as I tell you at once,' Bruce said sternly.

They came back, and Archie was silent and happy until Edith returned.

When she saw traces of sugar on his face and dress she said –

'Oh, Archie! What on earth did your father give you sugar for?'

'For talking about parrots,' said Archie.

Bruce's play

'EDITH,' said Bruce, 'come in here. I want to speak to you. Shut the door.'

She shut it, and stood waiting.

'Don't stand there. Come and sit down. . . . Now listen to me very seriously. I want to ask you a question.'

'How would you like me to be making about £5,000 a year – at least?'

'Need you ask?'

'And all by my own talent – not by anybody else's help.'

'It would be jolly,' she said, trying not to look doubtful.

'Jolly! I should think it would. Now I'll tell you my scheme – what I've made up my mind to do.'

'What?'

'I'm going to write a play.'

Edith controlled her expression, and said it was a very good idea.

'*Such* a play,' said Bruce. 'A really strong, powerful piece – all wit and cynicism like Bernard Shaw – *but*, full of heart and feeling and sentiment, and that sort of rot. It'll have all sorts of jolly fantastic ideas – like *Peter Pan* and *The*

Beloved Vagabond, but without the faults of Locke and Barrie - and it's going to be absolutely realistic and natural in parts - like the Sicilians, you know. However, I don't mind telling you that my model - you must have a model, more or less - is going to be Bernard Shaw. I like his style.'

'It's the most lovely idea I ever heard of. What theatre are you going to produce it at?'

'That depends. For some things I should prefer His Majesty's, but I'm rather fond of the Haymarket, too. However, if the terms were better, I might give it to Charlie Hawtrey, or even Alexander, if he offered me exceptionally good royalties.'

'Oh! Are you going to have it put up to auction?'

'Don't talk nonsense. What do you mean? No, I shall simply send a copy round to all the principal people and see what they say.'

He walked up and down the room once or twice.

'The reason I'm so determined not to let Bourchier have it is simply this: he doesn't realise my idea - he never could. Mind you, I believe he would do his best, but his Personality is against him. Do you see, Edith?'

'I see your point. But - '

'There's no reason why it shouldn't be quite as great a success as *The Merry Widow*.'

'Oh, is it going to be a comic opera?'

'Why, of course not. Don't I tell you it's to be a powerful play of real life.'

'Will you tell me the plot?'

He smiled rather fatuously. 'I'll tell you some of the plot, certainly, if you like - at least, I'll tell you how it's going to begin.'

'Do go on!' -

'Well, I must tell you it begins in a rather unconventional way - entirely different from most plays; but that'll make it all the more striking, and I *won't* alter it - mind that - not for anybody. Well, the curtain goes up, and you find two servants - do you see? - talking over their master and mistress. The maid - her name's Parker - is dusting the photographs and things, and she says to the manservant something about "The mistress does seem in a tantrum, doesn't she, Parker?" So he says - '

'But are they both called Parker?' asked Edith.

'Yes - no - of course not. I forgot; it's the man that's called Parker. But that isn't the point. Well, they talk, and gradually let out a little of the plot. Then two friends of the hero come in, and - oh, I can't bother to tell you any more now; but isn't it rather a good idea, eh? So new!'

'Capital! Splendid! Such a lovely original idea. I do wish you'd be quick and do it, Bruce.'

'I am being quick; but you mustn't be in too great a hurry; you must give me time.'

'Will it be ready in time for the season - I mean after Easter?'

'What! in a fortnight? How could they be ready to produce it in a fortnight, especially with the Easter holidays between? It won't be long, that I can promise you. I'm a quick worker.'

He waited a minute, and then said -

'You mustn't be depressed, Edith dear, if I get a little slating from some of the critics, you know. You can't expect them all to appreciate a new writer at once. And it really won't make any difference to the success if my play pleases the public, which I don't mind telling you I know it's sure to do; because, you see, it'll have all the good points and none of the bad ones of all the successful plays of the last six years. That's my dodge. That's how I do it.'

'I see.'

'Won't it be a joke when the governor and the mater are there on the first night? They'll be frightfully pleased. You must try and prevent the mater swaggering about it too much, you know. She's such a dear, she's sure to be absurdly proud of it. And it'll be a bit of a score off the governor in a way, too. He never would have thought I could do it, would he? And Raggett will be surprised, too. You must have a ripping new dress for the first night, Edith, old girl.'

'I think I shall have Liberty satin, dear – that new shade of blue – it wears better than Nattier. But I won't order it just yet. You haven't written the first scene, have you?'

'The first scene? No! Plays aren't done like that. The chief thing about a play like this is to get a scenario.'

'Oh! Isn't that where the people sit?'

'Don't be ridiculous! You're thinking of the auditorium. I mean the skeleton of the play. That's what I shall send round to the managers. They can see what it's going to be like at once.'

'How many acts will it be?'

'Four.'

'And have you settled on the name?'

'Yes, as a matter of fact I have settled on a name; but don't you go giving it away. It's rather an original name. It would do if I developed the comedy interest just the same and just as well as if I made the chief point the tragic part. It's going to be called *You Never Know*. Good name, isn't it?'

'It's a splendid name. But isn't it a tiny bit like something else?'

'How unsympathetic you are! The fact is you don't understand. That's what it is.'

'Oh, I do sympathise immensely, Bruce, and I'm sure you'll have a great success. What fun it will be! Are you going to work at it this afternoon?'

'Why, no! not *this* afternoon. I'm rather tired out with thinking. I think I shall go and look in at the club.'

Hyacinth waits

'HE'S coming this afternoon, Anne,' Hyacinth said. 'See that I'm really alone today – I mean that I'm out to everyone.'

'You think, then, that he really will propose today?'

'Don't be so horribly explicit. Don't you think his having to go the other day – because of Lady Cannon – would lead to a sort of crisis? I mean, either he wouldn't come here again, or else – '

'I suppose it would,' said Anne. 'At least, it would if he had some glimmering of his own intentions. But he's in such a very undecided state.'

'Well, don't let's worry about his intentions. At any rate, he's coming to see me. The question is, what shall I wear?'

'It doesn't matter in the least. You attach a ridiculous amount of importance to dress.'

'Perhaps; but I must wear *something*. So what shall it be?'

'Well, if you want to look prepared for a proposal – so as to give him a sort of hint – you'd better wear your pale mauve dress. It's becoming, and it looks festive and spring-like.'

'Oh, Anne! Why, it's ever so much too smart! It would be quite ridiculous. Just like you, advising pale mauve *crêpe de Chine* and Irish lace for a quiet visit in the afternoon from a friend!'

'Oh! all right. Then wear your blue tailor-made dress – and the little boots with the cloth tops.'

'Oh, good heavens, Anne! I'm not going for a bicycle ride. Because I'm not got up for a garden-party, it doesn't follow I must be dressed for mountain-climbing. Cecil hates sensible-looking clothes.'

'Then I should think anything you've got would do. Or do you want to get a new dress?'

'Of course I want to get a new dress, but not for this afternoon. It wouldn't be possible. Besides, I don't think it's a good plan to wear something different every time you see a person. It looks so extravagant.'

'Wear your black and white, then.'

'No, it isn't *intime* enough, and the material's too rough – it's a hard dress.'

'Oh! Funny, I had the impression you had more clothes than you knew what to do with, and you don't seem to have anything fit to wear.'

'Why, of course, I shall wear my blue voile. How on earth could I wear anything else? How silly you are, Anne!'

'Well, if you knew that all the time, why did you ask me?'

'Are there plenty of flowers in the studio?'

'Yes; but I'll get some more if you like.'

'No, no; don't have too many. It looks too *arranged*.'

She looked at the clock.

'It won't be five just yet,' said Anne. 'It's only eleven.'

'Yes; that's the awful part. What on earth shall I do till then?'

'Whatever I suggested, you would do the reverse.'

'Shall I go for a long drive in the motor?'

'That's a good idea.'

'But it's a very windy day, and I might get neuralgia – not feel up to the mark.'

'So you might. I think, perhaps, the best thing for you would be to have your hair waved.'

'How can I sit still to have my hair waved? Besides, it makes it look too stiff – like a hairdresser's dummy.'

'Ah! there is that. Then why not do something useful – go and be manicured?'

'I'm afraid I shouldn't have the patience today.'

'I suppose what you'd really like,' said Anne, 'would be to see Edith Ottley.'

'No, I shouldn't. Not till tomorrow. I don't want to see anybody,' said Hyacinth.

'Well, all right. I'm going out.'

'Oh, but I can't bear to be alone.'

'Then I scarcely see . . . '

'This afternoon especially, Anne. You must stay with me till about a quarter of an hour before I expect him. The horrible agony of waiting is so frightful! It makes me feel so ill. But I don't want you to stay beyond the time I expect him, in case he's late. Because then I suffer so much that I couldn't bear you to see it.'

'I see. How jolly it must be to be in love! You *do* seem to have a good time.'

'When one has the slightest hope, Anne, it's simply too awful. Of course, if one hasn't, one bears it.'

'And if one has no encouragement, I suppose one gets over it?'

'I have a presentiment that everything will be all right today,' said Hyacinth. 'Is that a bad sign?'

CHAPTER EIGHTEEN

'There are no good signs, in your present state,' answered Anne.

It was about half-past four, and Hyacinth in the blue dress, was sitting in the studio, where she could see both the window and the clock. Anne, by the fire, was watching her.

'You seem very fairly calm, Hyacinth.'

'I am calm,' she said. 'I am; quite calm. Except that my heart is beating so fast that I can hardly breathe, that I have horrible kinds of shivers and a peculiar feeling in my throat, I'm quite all right. Now, just fancy if I had to pretend I wasn't in suspense! If I had no-one to confide in! ... Do you think he's mistaken the day? Do you think he thinks it's Thursday instead of Tuesday?'

'That's not likely.'

'I'm glad I feel so cool and calm. How ashamed I should be if he ever knew that I was so agitated!'

'Who knows, perhaps he's feeling as uncomfortable as you are?'

'Oh, no, no! There's no hope of that. ... Will he telephone and put it off, do you think, at the last minute?'

'I shouldn't think so.'

'Are there any little pink cakes?'

'Heaps. Far more than will ever be eaten.'

'Now, don't talk to me, Anne. I'm going to read for a quarter of an hour.'

She took up a novel and read two pages, then looked up at the clock and turned pale.

'It's five. Is that clock fast?'

'No; listen, the church clock's striking. Good-bye.'

Anne went, and Hyacinth kissed her hand to her and arranged her hair in the mirror. She then sat down and resolved to be perfectly quiet.

Ten minutes slowly ticked away, then Hyacinth went to the window, saying to herself that it was an unlucky thing to do. She did not remain there long, then walked round and round the room. Several cabs passed, each of which she thought was going to stop. Then she sat down again, looking cool and smiling, carelessly holding a book. . . . Each time the cab passed. It was half-past five, rather late under the circumstances. She was angry. She resolved to be very cold to him when he first came in, or - no, she wouldn't be cold, she would pretend she didn't know he was late - hadn't noticed it; or she would chaff him about it, and say she would never wait again. She took the letter from her pocket and read it again. It said-

'DEAR MISS VERNEY,

'May I come and see you at five o'clock tomorrow afternoon?

'Yours,

'CECIL REEVE.'

Its very brevity had shown it was something urgent, but perhaps he would come to break off their friendship; since the awkwardness of Lady Cannon's visit, he must have been thinking that things couldn't go on like this. Then she began to recapitulate details, arguing to herself with all the cold, hard logic of passion.

At Lord Selsey's afternoon she had given herself away by her anger, by the jealousy she showed, and had told him never to come and see her again. Immediately after that had been their meeting at the National Gallery, where Cecil had followed her and sought her out. Then they had those two delightful walks in Kensington Gardens, in which he had really seemed to 'like' her so much. Then the pleasant intimate little lunch, after which Lady Cannon had called.... In the course of these meetings he had told her that he and Mrs Raymond had quarrelled, that she would never see him again. She had felt that he was drifting to her.... How strangely unlike love affairs in books hers had been! In all respectable novels it was the man who fell in love first. No-one knew by experience better than Hyacinth how easily that might happen, how very often it did. But she, who was proud, reserved, and a little shy with all her expansiveness, had simply fallen hopelessly in love with him at first sight. It was at that party at the Burlingtons. She realised now that she had practically thought of nothing else since. Probably she was spoilt, for she had not foreseen any difficulty; she had had always far more admirers than she cared for, and her difficulties had usually been in trying to get rid of them. He seemed to like her, but that was all. Mrs Raymond was, of course, the reason, but Mrs Raymond was over. She looked up at the clock again.

Ten minutes to six. Perhaps he had made it up with Mrs Raymond? ... For the next ten minutes she suffered extraordinary mental tortures, then her anger consoled her a little. He had treated her too rudely! It was amazing - extraordinary! He was not worth caring for. At any rate, it showed he didn't care for her.... If it was some unavoidable accident, couldn't he have telephoned or telegraphed? ... No; it was one of those serious things that one can only write about. He was with Mrs Raymond, she felt sure of that. But Mrs Raymond didn't like him.... Perhaps, after all, he had only been detained in some extraordinary way, she might hear directly ...

She went up to her room, and was slightly consoled for the moment to find the clock there five minutes slower than the one in the drawing-room. She again arranged her hair and went into the hall, where she found two or three cards of people who had called, and been told she was out – an irritating detail – for nothing! Then she went back to the studio.

Even to be in the place where she had been waiting for him was something, it gave her a little illusion that he would be here again. . . . Could he really be an hour and a quarter late? It was just possible.

She heard a ring. Every sign of anxiety disappeared from her face. She was beaming, and got back into the old attitude, holding the book. She could hear her heart beating while there was some parley in the hall. Unable to bear it any more, she opened the door. It was someone with a parcel.

'What is it?'

'It's only the new candle-shades, miss. Shall I bring them in for you to see?'

'No, thank you. . . . '

Candle-shades!

She put her hands over her eyes and summoned all her pride. Probably the very butler and her maid knew perfectly well she had been waiting at home alone for Mr Reeve. She cared absolutely nothing what they thought; but she felt bitter, revengeful to him. It was cruel.

Why did she care so much? She remembered letters and scenes with other people – people whose sufferings about her she felt always inclined to laugh at. She couldn't believe in it. Love in books had always seemed to her, although intensely interesting, just a trifle absurd. She couldn't realise it till now.

Another ring. Perhaps it was he after all! . . .

The same position. The book, the bright blue eyes . . .

The door opened; Anne came in. It was striking seven o'clock.

Eugenia

MEANWHILE Cecil had received a note from his uncle, asking him to go and see him. He decided he would do so on his way to see Hyacinth.

For many days now he had not seen Mrs Raymond. She had answered no letters, and been always 'out' to him.

As he walked along, he wondered what had become of her, and tried to think he didn't care.

'I have news for you, Cecil,' said his uncle; 'but, first, you really have made up your mind, haven't you, to try your luck with Hyacinth? What a pretty perfumed name it is – just like her.'

'I suppose I shall try.'

'Good. I'm delighted to hear it. Then in a very short time I shall hear that you're as happy as I am.'

'As you, Uncle Ted?'

'Look at this house, Cecil. It's full of Things; it wants looking after. I want looking after. . . . I am sure you wouldn't mind – wouldn't be vexed to hear I was going to marry again?'

'Rather not. I'm glad. It must be awfully lonely here sometimes. But I am surprised, I must say. Everybody looks upon you as a confirmed widower, Uncle Ted.'

'Well, so I have been a confirmed widower – for eighteen years. I think that's long enough.'

Cecil waited respectfully.

Then his uncle said abruptly –

'I saw Mrs Raymond yesterday.'

Cecil started and blushed.

'Did you? Where did you meet her?'

'I didn't meet her. I went to see her. I spent two hours with her.'

Cecil stared in silent amazement.

'It was my fourth visit,' said Lord Selsey.

'You spent all that time talking over my affairs?'

His uncle gave a slight smile. 'Indeed not, Cecil. After the first few minutes of the first visit, frankly, we said very little about you.'

'But I don't understand.'

'I've been all this time trying to persuade her to something – against her judgement. I've been trying to persuade her to marry.'

'To marry me?'

'No. To marry me. And I've succeeded.'

'I congratulate you,' said Cecil, in a cold, hard voice.

'You're angry, my boy. It's very natural; but let me explain to you how it happened.'

He paused, and then went on: 'Of course, for years I've wished for the right woman here. But I never saw her. I thought I never should. That day she came here – the musical party – the moment I looked at her, I saw that she was meant for me, not for you.'

'I call it a beastly shame,' said Cecil.

'It isn't. It's absolutely right. You know perfectly well she never would have cared for you in the way you wished.'

Cecil could not deny that, but he said sarcastically –

'So you fell in love with her at first sight?'

'Oh no, I didn't. I'm not in love with her now. But I think she's beautiful. I mean she has a beautiful soul – she has atmosphere, she has something that I need. I could live in the same house with her in perfect harmony for ever. I could teach her to understand my Things. She does already by instinct.'

'You're marrying her as a kind of custodian for your collection?'

'A great deal, of course. And, then, I couldn't marry a young girl. It would be ridiculous. A society woman – a regular beauty – would jar on me and irritate me. She would think herself more important than my pictures.'

Cecil could hardly help a smile, angry as he was.

'And Mrs Raymond,' went on Lord Selsey, 'is delightfully unworldly – and yet sensible. Of course, she's not a bit in love with me either. But she likes me awfully, and I persuaded her. It was all done by argument.'

'I could never persuade her,' said Cecil bitterly.

'Of course not. She has such a sense of form. She saw the incongruity. . . . I needn't ask you to forgive me, old boy. I know, of course, there's nothing to forgive. You've got over your fancy, or you will very soon. I haven't injured you in any sort of way, and I didn't take her away from you. She's ten years older than you, and nine years younger than me. . . . You're still my heir just the same. This will make no difference, and you'll soon be reconciled. I'm sure of that.'

'Of course, I'm not such a brute as not to be glad, for her,' said Cecil slowly, after a slight struggle. 'It seems a bit rough, though, at first.' He held out his hand.

'Thanks, dear old boy. You see I'm right. You can't be angry with me. . . . You see it's a peculiar case. It won't be like an ordinary marriage, a young married couple and so on, nor a *mariage de convenance*, either, in the ordinary sense. Here are two lonely people intending to live solitary lives. Suddenly, you – *most* kindly, I must say – introduce us. I, with my great experience and my instinctive *flair*, see immediately that this is the right woman in the right place. I bother her until she consents – and there you are.'

'I hope you'll be happy.'

They shook hands in silence, and Cecil got into a hansom and drove straight to Mrs Raymond's. He was furious.

While Hyacinth, whose very existence he had forgotten in the shock and anger of this news, was feeling, with the agonising clairvoyance of love, that Cecil was with Mrs Raymond, she was perfectly right.

Today Eugenia was at home, and did not refuse to see him.

'I see you know,' she remarked coolly as he came in.

Cecil had controlled his emotion when with his uncle, but seeing Mrs Raymond again in the dismal little old drawing-room dealt him a terrible blow. He saw, only too vividly, the picture of his suave, exquisite uncle, standing out against this muddled, confused background, in the midst of decoration which was one long disaster and furniture that was one desperate failure. To think that the owner of Selsey House had spent hours here! The thought was jealous agony.

'I must congratulate you,' he said coldly.

'Thank you, Cecil.'

'I thought you were never going to marry again?' he said sarcastically.

'I never do, as a rule. But this is an exception. And it isn't going to be like an ordinary marriage. We shall each have complete freedom. He persuaded me – to look after that lovely house. It will give me an object in life. And besides, Cecil,' she was laughing, 'think – to be your aunt! The privilege!'

He seized her by the shoulders. She laughed still more, and put one hand on the bell, at which he released her. He walked away so violently that he knocked down a screen.

'There, that will do,' said Eugenia, picking it up. 'You've made your little scene, and shown your little temper, and that's enough. Sit down,' she commanded.

Cecil sat down, feeling a complete fool.

'Look here. I daresay that it's a little annoying for you, at first, especially as you introduced us; but really, when you come to think it over, there's no law of etiquette, or any other that I know of, which compels me to refuse the uncle of a young man who has done me the honour to like me. Oh, Cecil, don't be absurd!'

'Are you in love with him?'

'No. But I think he will be very pleasant – not worrying and fidgeting – so calm and kind. I refused at first, Cecil. People always want what they can't get, and if it's any satisfaction to you, I don't mind confessing that I have had, for years, a perfect mania for somebody else. A hopeless case for at least three reasons: he's married, he's in love with someone else (not even counting his wife, who counts a great deal) and, if he hadn't either of these preoccupations, he would never look at me. So I've given it up. I've made up my mind to forget it. Your uncle will help me, and give me something else to think about.'

'Who was the man?' Cecil asked. It was some slight satisfaction to know that she also had had a wasted affection.

'Why should I tell you? I shall not tell you. Well, I will tell you. It's Sir Charles Cannon.'

'Old Cannon?'

'Yes; it was a sort of mad hero-worship. I never could account for it. I always thought him the most wonderful person. He hasn't the faintest idea of it, and never will; and now don't let's speak of him again.'

The name reminded Cecil of Hyacinth. He started violently, remembering his appointment. What must she have thought of him?

'Good-bye, Eugenia,' he said.

As he held her hand he felt, in a sense, as if it was in some strange way, after all, a sort of triumph for him, a score that Lord Selsey had appreciated her so wonderfully.

As he left the house it struck seven. What was he to do about Hyacinth?

That evening Hyacinth received a large basket of flowers and a letter, in which Cecil threw himself on her mercy, humbling himself to the earth, and imploring her to let him come and explain and apologise next day. He entreated her to be kind enough to let him off waiting till a conventional hour, and to allow him to call in the morning.

He received a kind, forgiving answer, and then spent the most miserable night of his life.

Bruce has influenza

ALL women love news of whatever kind; even bad news gives them merely a feeling of pleasurable excitement, unless it is something that affects them or those they love personally.

Edith was no exception to the rule, but she knew that Bruce, on the contrary, disliked it; if it were bad he was angry and said it served the people right, while if it were good he thought they didn't deserve it and disapproved strongly. Bruce spent a great deal of his time and energy in disapproving; generally of things and people that were no concern of his. As is usually the case, this high moral attitude was caused by envy. Bruce would have been much surprised to hear it, but envy was the keynote of his character, and he saw everything that surrounded him through its vague mist.

All newspapers made him furious. He regarded everything in them as a personal affront; from the fashionable intelligence, describing political dinners in Berkeley Square or dances in Curzon Street, where he thought he should have been present in the important character of host, to notices of plays - plays which he felt he could have written so well. Even sensational thefts irritated him; perhaps he unconsciously fancied that the stolen things (Crown jewels, and so forth) should by rights have been his, and that he would have known how to take care of them. 'Births, Marriages, and Deaths' annoyed him intensely. If he read that Lady So-and-So had twin sons, the elder of whom would be heir to the title and estates, he was disgusted to think of the injustice that he hadn't a title and estates for Archie to inherit, and he mentally held the newly-arrived children very cheap, feeling absolutely certain that they would compare most unfavourably with his boy, excepting, of course, in the accident of their worldly circumstances. Also, although he was proud of having married, and fond of Edith, descriptions of 'Society Weddings of the Week' drove him absolutely wild – wild to think that he and Edith, who deserved it, hadn't had an Archbishop, choirboys, guardsmen with crossed swords to walk under, and an amethyst brooch from a member of the Royal Family at their wedding. New discoveries in science pained him, for he knew that he would have thought of them long before, and carried them out much better, had he only had the time.

Bruce had had influenza, and when Edith came in with her news, she could not at once make up her mind to tell him, fearing his anger.

He was lying on the sofa with the paper, grumbling at the fuss made about the Sicilian players, of whom he was clearly jealous.

She sat down by his side and agreed with him.

'I'm much worse since you went out. You know the usual results of influenza, don't you? Heart failure, or nervous depression liable to lead to suicide.'

'But you're much better, dear. Dr Braithwaite said it was wonderful how quickly you threw it off.'

'Threw it off! Yes, but that's only because I have a marvellous constitution and great will-power. If I happened to have had less strength and vitality, I might easily have been dead by now. I wish you'd go and fetch me some cigarettes, dear. I have none left.'

She got up and went to the door.

'What are you fidgeting about, Edith?' said he. '*Can't* you keep still? It's not at all good for a convalescent to have a restless person with him.'

'Why, I was only going to fetch – '

'I know you were; but you should learn repose, dear. First you go out all the morning, and when you come home you go rushing about the room.'

She sat down again and decided to tell him.

'You'll be glad to hear,' she said, 'that Hyacinth and Cecil Reeve are engaged. They are to be married in the autumn.'

Guessing she expected him to display interest, he answered irritably –

'I don't care. It has nothing to do with me.'

'No, of course not.'

'I never heard anything so idiotic as having a wedding in the autumn. A most beastly time, I think – November fogs.'

'I heard something else,' said Edith, 'which surprised me much more. Fancy, Lord Selsey's going to be married – to Mrs Raymond. Isn't that extraordinary?'

'Lord Selsey – a widower! Disgusting! I thought he pretended be so fond of his first wife.'

'He was, dear, I believe. But she died eighteen years ago, and – '

'Instead of telling me all this tittle-tattle it would be much better if you did as I asked you, Edith, and fetched me the cigarettes. I've asked you several times. Of course I don't want to make a slave of you. I'm not one of those men who want their wives to be a drudge. But, after all, they're only in the next room. It isn't a *very* hard task! And I'm very weak, or I'd go myself.'

She ran out and brought them back before he could stop her again.

'Who is this Mrs Raymond?' he then asked.

'Oh, she's a very nice woman – a widow. Really quite suitable in age to Lord Selsey. Not young. She's not a bit pretty and not in his set at all. He took the most violent fancy to her at first sight, it seems. She had vowed never to marry again, but he persuaded her.'

'Well,' said Bruce, striking a match, 'they didn't consult me! They must go their own way. I'm sorry for them, of course. Lord Selsey always seemed to me a very agreeable chap, so it seems rather a pity. At the same time, I suppose it's a bad thing – in the worldly sense – for Reeve, and *that's* satisfactory.'

'Oh! I think he's all right,' said Edith, and she smiled thoughtfully.

'You're always smiling, Edith,' he complained. 'Particularly when I have something to annoy me.'

'Am I? I believe I read in the "Answers to Correspondents" in *Home Chirps* that a wife should always have a bright smile if her husband seemed depressed.'

'Good heavens! How awful! Why, it would be like living with a Cheshire cat!'

Edith warmly began to defend herself from the accusation, when Bruce stopped her by saying that his temperature had gone up, and asking her to fetch the clinical thermometer.

Having snatched it from her and tried it, he turned pale and said in a hollow voice –

'Telephone to Braithwaite. At once. Say it's urgent. Poor little Edith!'

CHAPTER TWENTY

'What is it?' she cried in a frightened voice.

'I'd better not tell you,' he said, trying to hide it.

'Tell me – oh! tell me!'

'It's a hundred and nineteen. Now, don't waste time. You meant no harm, dear, but you worried and excited me. It isn't your fault. Don't blame yourself. Of course, you *would* do it.'

'Oh, I know what it is,' cried Edith. 'I dipped it in boiling water before I gave it to you.'

'Idiot! You might have broken it!' said Bruce.

The explanation seemed to annoy him very much; nevertheless he often referred afterwards to the extraordinary way his temperature used to jump about, which showed what a peculiarly violent, virulent, dangerous form of influenza he had had, and how wonderful it was he had thrown it off, in spite of Edith's inexperienced, not to say careless, nursing, entirely by his own powerful will and indomitable courage.

'Engaged'

LADY CANNON sat in her massive, florid clothes, that always seemed part of her massive, florid furniture, and to have the same expression of violent, almost ominous conventionality, without the slightest touch of austerity to tone it down. Her throat and figure seemed made solely to show off dog-collars and long necklaces; her head seemed constructed specially for the wearing of a dark red royal fringe and other ornaments. Today she was in her most cheerful and condescending mood, in fact she was what is usually called in a good temper. It was a great satisfaction to her that Hyacinth was at last settled; and she decided to condone the rather wilful way in which the engagement had been finally arranged without reference to her. With the touch of somewhat sickly sentiment common to most hard women, she took great pleasure in a wedding (if it were only moderately a suitable one), and was prepared to be arch and sympathetic with the engaged couple whom she expected today to pay her a formal visit.

She was smiling to herself as she turned a bracelet on her left wrist, and wondered if she and Sir Charles need really run to a tiara, since after all they weren't Hyacinth's parents, and was wishing they could get off with giving her a certain piece of old lace that had been in the family for years, and could never be arranged to wear, when Sir Charles came in.

'Ah, Charles, that's right. I wish you to be here to welcome Hyacinth and her fiancé. I'm expecting them directly.'

'I can't possibly be here,' he said. 'I have a most urgent appointment. I've done all the right things. I've written to them, and gone to see Hyacinth, and we've asked them to dinner. No more is necessary. Of course, let them understand that I – I quite approve, and all that. And I really think that's quite enough.'

He spoke rather irritably.

'Really, Charles, how morose you've grown. One would think you disliked to see young people happy together. I always think it's such a pretty sight. Especially as it's a regular love match.'

'No doubt; no doubt. Charming! But I have an appointment; I must go at once.'

'With whom, may I ask?'

'With St Leonards,' he answered unblushingly.

'Oh! Oh well, of course, they'll understand you couldn't keep the Duke waiting. I'll mention it; I'll explain. I shall see a little more of Hyacinth just now, Charles. It'll be the right thing. An engaged girl ought to be chaperoned by a connection of the family – of some weight. Not a person like that Miss Yeo. I shall arrange to drive out with Hyacinth and advise her about her trousseau, and ...'

'Yes; do as you like, but spare me the details.'

Lady Cannon sighed.

'Ah, Charles, you have no romance. Doesn't the sight of these happy young people bring back the old days?'

The door shut. Lady Cannon was alone.

'He has no soul,' she said to herself, using a tiny powder-puff.

The young people, as they were now called, had had tea with her in her magnificent drawing-room. She had said and done everything that was obvious, kind, and tedious. She had held Hyacinth's hand, and shaken a forefinger at Cecil, and then she explained to them that it would be much more the right thing now for them to meet at her house, rather than at Hyacinth's - a recommendation which they accepted with complete (apparent) gravity, and in fact she seemed most anxious to take entire possession of them - to get the credit of them, as it were, as a social sensation.

'And now,' she said, 'what do you think I'm going to do? If you won't think me very rude' (threatening forefinger again), 'I'm going to leave you alone for a little while. I shan't be very long; but I have to write a letter, and so on, and when I come back I shall have on my bonnet, and I'll drive Hyacinth home.'

'It's most awfully kind of you, Auntie, but Cecil's going to drive me back.'

'No, no, no! I insist, I insist! This dear child has been almost like a daughter to me, you know,' pressing a lace-edged little handkerchief, scented with Ess Bouquet, to a dry little eye. 'You mustn't take her away all at once! Will you be very angry if I leave you?' and laughing in what she supposed to be an entirely charming manner, she glided, as though on castors, in her fringed, embroidered, brocaded dress from the room.

'Isn't she magnificent?' said Cecil.

'You know she has a reputation for being remarkable for sound sense,' said Hyacinth.

CHAPTER TWENTY-ONE

'Well, she's shown it at last!'

She laughed.

He took a stroll round the room. It was so high, so enormous, with so much satin on the walls, so many looking-glasses, so much white paint, so many cabinets full of Dresden china, that it recalled, by the very extremity of the contrast of its bright hideousness, that other ugly, dismal little room, also filled with false gods, of a cheap and very different kind, in which he had had so much poignant happiness.

'Hyacinth,' he said, rather quaintly, 'do you know what I'm doing? I want to kiss you, and I'm looking for a part of the room in which it wouldn't be blasphemous!'

'You can't find one, Cecil. I couldn't - here. And her leaving us alone makes it all the more impossible.'

The girl was seated on a stiff, blue silk settee, padded and buttoned, and made in a peculiar form in which three people can sit, turning their backs to one another. She leant her sweet face on her hand, her elbow on the peculiar kind of mammoth pincushion that at once combined and separated the three seats. (It had been known formerly as a 'lounge' - a peculiarly unsuitable name, as it was practically impossible not to sit in it bolt upright.)

Cecil stood opposite and looked down at her.

Happiness, and the hope of happiness, had given her beauty a different character. There was something touching, troubling about her. It seemed to him that she had everything: beauty, profane and spiritual; deep blue eyes, in which he could read devotion; womanly tenderness, and a flower-like complexion; a perfect figure, and a beautiful soul. He could be proud of her before the world, and he could delight in her in private. She appealed, he thought, to everything in a man - his vanity, his intellect, and his senses. The better he knew her, the more exquisite qualities he found in her. She was sweet, clever, good, and she vibrated to his every look. She was sensitive, and passionate. She was adorable. He was too fortunate! Then why did he think of a pale, tired, laughing face, with the hair dragged off the forehead, and Japanese eyes? . . . What folly!

It was a recurring obsession.

'Cecil, what are you thinking about?'

'Of you.'

'Do you love me? Will you always love me? Are you happy?'

He made no answer, but kissed the questions from her lips, and from his own heart.

So Lady Cannon, after rattling the handle of the door, came in in her bonnet, and found them, as she had expected. Then she sent Cecil away and drove Hyacinth home, talking without ceasing during the drive of bridesmaids, choral services, bishops, travelling-bags, tea-gowns, and pretty little houses in Mayfair.

Hyacinth did not hear a single word she said, so, as Lady Cannon answered all her own questions in the affirmative, and warmly agreed with all her own remarks, she quite enjoyed herself, and decided that Hyacinth had immensely improved, and that Ella was to come back for the wedding.

The strange behaviour of Anne

IT was a spring-like, warm-looking, deceptive day, with a bright sun and a cold east wind.

Anne sat, a queer-looking figure, in an unnecessary mackintosh and a golf-cap, on a bench in a large open space in Hyde Park, looking absently at some shabby sheep. She had come here to be alone, to think. Soon she would be alone as much as she liked – much more. She had appeared quite sympathetically cheerful, almost jaunty, since her friend's engagement. She could not bear anyone to know her real feelings. Hyacinth had been most sweet, warmly affectionate to her; Cecil delightful. They had asked her to go and stay with them. Lady Cannon had graciously said, 'I suppose you will be looking out for another situation now, Miss Yeo?' and others had supposed she would go back to her father's Rectory, for a time, at any rate.

Today the wedding had been definitely fixed, and she had come out to give way to the bitterness of her solitude.

She realised that she had not the slightest affection for anyone in the world except Hyacinth, and that no-one had any for her, on anything like the same scale.

Anne was a curious creature. Her own family had always been absolutely indifferent to her, and from her earliest youth she had hated and despised all men that she had known. Sir Charles Cannon was the only human being for whom she felt a little sympathy, instinctively knowing that under all his amiable congratulations he disliked Hyacinth's marriage almost as much as she did, and in the same way.

All the strength of her feelings and affections, then, which in the ordinary course would have gone in other channels, Anne had lavished on Hyacinth. She adored her as if she had been her own child. She worshipped her like an idol. As a matter of fact, being quite independent financially, it was not as a paid companion at all that she had lived with her, though she chose to appear in that capacity. And, besides Hyacinth herself, Anne had, in a most superlative degree, enjoyed the house, her little authority, the way she stood between Hyacinth and all tedious little practical matters. Like many a woman who was a virago at heart, Anne had a perfect passion for domestic matters, for economy, for managing a house. Of course she had always known that the pretty heiress was sure to marry, but she hoped the evil day would be put off, and somehow it annoyed her to such an acute extent because Hyacinth was so particularly pleased with the young man.

As she told Anne every thought, and never dreamt of concealing any nuance or shade of her sentiments, Anne had suffered a good deal.

It vexed her particularly that Hyacinth fancied Cecil so unusual, while she was very certain that there were thousands and thousands of good-looking young men in England in the same position who had the same education, who were precisely like him. There was not a pin to choose between them. How many photographs in groups Cecil had shown them, when she and Hyacinth went to tea at his rooms! Cecil in a group at Oxford, in an eleven, as a boy at school, and so forth! While Hyacinth delightedly recognised Cecil, Anne wondered how on earth she could tell one from the other. Of course, he was not a bad sort. He was rather clever, and not devoid of a sense of humour, but the fault Anne really found with him, besides his taking his privileges so much as a matter of course, was that there was nothing, really, to find fault with. Had he been ugly and stupid, she could have minded it less.

Now what should she do? Of course she must remain with Hyacinth till the marriage, but she was resolved not to go to the wedding, although she had promised to do so. Both Hyacinth and Cecil really detested the vulgarity of a showy fashionable wedding as much as she did, and it was to be moderated, toned down as much as possible. But Anne couldn't stand it – any of it – and she wasn't going to try.

As she sat there, wrapped up in her egotistic anguish, two young people, probably a shop-girl and her young man, passed, sauntering along, holding hands, and swinging their arms. Anne thought that they were, if anything, less odious than the others, but the stupidity of their happiness irritated her, and she got up to go back.

She felt tired, and though it was not far, she decided, with her usual unnecessary economy, to go by omnibus down Park Lane.

As she got out and felt for the key in her pocket, she thought how soon she would no longer be able to go into her paradise and find the lovely creature waiting to confide in her, how even now the lovely creature was in such a dream of preoccupied happiness that, quick as she usually was, she was now perfectly blind to her friend's jealousy. And, indeed, Anne concealed it very well. It was not ordinary jealousy either. She was very far from envying Hyacinth. She only hated parting with her.

As she passed the studio she heard voices, and looked in, just as she was, with a momentary desire to *gêner* them.

Of course they got up, Hyacinth blushing and laughing, and entreated her to come in.

She sat there a few minutes, hoping to chill their high spirits, then abruptly left them in the middle of a sentence.

At dinner that evening she appeared quite as usual. She had taken a resolution.

Bruce convalescent

'IT'S very important,' said Bruce, 'that I don't see too many people at a time. You must arrange the visitors carefully. Who is coming this afternoon?'

'I don't know of anyone, except perhaps your mother, and Mr Raggett.'

'Ah! Well, I can't see them both at once.'

'Really? Why not?'

'*Why* not? What a question! Because it would be a terrible fatigue for me. I shouldn't be able to stand it. In fact I'm not sure that I ought to see Raggett at all.'

'Don't, then. Leave a message to say that after all you didn't feel strong enough.'

'But, if we do that, won't he think it rather a shame, poor chap? As I said he could come, doesn't it seem rather hard lines for him to come all this way – it is a long distance, mind you – and then see nobody?'

'Well, I can see him.'

Bruce looked up suspiciously.

'Oh, you want to see him, do you? Alone?'

'Don't be silly, Bruce. I would much rather not see him.'

'Indeed, and why not? I really believe you look down on him because he's my friend.'

'Not a bit. Well, he won't be angry; you can say that you had a relapse, or something, and were not well enough to see him.'

'Nothing of the sort. It would be very good for me; a splendid change to have a little intellectual talk with a man of the world. I've had too much women's society lately. I'm sick of it. Ring the bell, Edith.'

'Of course I will, Bruce, but what for? Is it anything I can do?'

'I want you to ring for Bennett to pass me my tonic.'

'Really, Bruce, it's at your elbow.' She laughed.

'I suppose I've changed a good deal since my illness,' said he looking in the glass with some complacency.

'You don't look at all bad, dear.'

'I know I'm better; but sometimes, just as people are recovering, they suddenly have a frightful relapse. Braithwaite told me I would have to be careful for some time.'

'How long do you suppose he meant?'

'I don't know – five or six years, I suppose. It's the heart. That's what's so risky in influenza.'

'But he said your heart was all right.'

'Ah, so he thinks. Doctors don't know everything. Or perhaps it's what he *says*. It would never do to tell a heart patient he was in immediate danger, Edith; why, he might die on the spot from the shock.'

'Yes, dear; but, excuse my saying so, would he have taken me aside and told me you were perfectly well, and that he wouldn't come to see you again, if you were really in a dangerous state?'

'Very possibly. I don't know that I've so very much confidence in Braithwaite. I practically told him so. At least I suggested to him, when he seemed so confident about my recovery, that he should have a consultation. I thought it only fair to give him every chance.'

'And what did he say?'

'He didn't seem to see it. Just go and get the cards, Edith, that have been left during my illness. It's the right thing for me to write to everyone, and thank them for their kindness.'

'But there are no cards, dear.'

'No cards?'

'You see, people who knew you were ill inquired by telephone, except your mother, and she never leaves a card.'

He seemed very disgusted.

'That's it,' he said. 'That's just like life; "laugh, and the world laughs with you; weep, and you weep alone!" Get out of the running, and drop aside, and you're forgotten. And I'm a fairly popular man, too; yet I might have died like a dog in this wretched little flat, and not a card. – What's that ring?'

'It must be your mother.'

Bruce leant back on the sofa in a feeble attitude, gave Edith directions to pull the blinds a little way down, and had a vase of roses placed by his side.

Then his mother was shown in.

'Well, how is the interesting invalid? Dear boy, how well you look! How perfectly splendid you look!'

'Hush, Mother,' said Bruce, with a faint smile, and in a very low voice. 'Sit down, and be a little quiet. Yes, I'm much better, and getting on well; but I can't stand much yet.'

'Dear, dear! And what did the doctor say?' she asked Edith.

'He won't come any more,' said Edith.

'Isn't he afraid you will be rushing out to the office too soon – overworking? Oh well, Edith will see that you take care of yourself. Where's little Archie?'

'Go and see him in the nursery,' said Bruce, almost in a whisper. 'I can't stand a lot of people in here.'

'Archie's out,' said Edith.

There was another ring.

'That's how it goes on all day long,' said Bruce. 'I don't know how it's got about, I'm sure. People never cease calling! It's an infernal nuisance.'

'Well, it's nice to know you're not neglected,' said his mother.

'Neglected? Why, it's been more like a crowded reception than an invalid's room.'

'It's Mr Raggett,' said Edith; 'I heard his voice. Will you see him or not, dear?'

'Yes. Presently. Take him in the other room, and when the mater goes he can come in here.'

'I'm going now,' said Mrs Ottley; 'you mustn't have a crowd. But really, Bruce, you're better than you think.'

'Ah, I'm glad you think so. I should hate you to be anxious.'

'Your father wanted to know when you would be able to go to the office again.'

'That entirely depends. I may be strong enough in a week or two, but I promised Braithwaite not to be rash for Edith's sake. Well, good-bye, Mother, if you must go.'

She kissed him, left a box of soldiers for Archie and murmured to Edith –

'What an angel Bruce is! So patient and brave. Perfectly well, of course. He has been for a week. He'll go on thinking himself ill for a year – the dear pet, the image of his father! If I were you, Edith I think I should get ill too; it will be the only way to get him out. What a perfect wife you are!'

'I should like to go back with you a little,' said Edith.

CHAPTER TWENTY-THREE

'Well, can't you? I'm going to Harrod's, of course. I'm always going to Harrod's; it's the only place I ever do go. As Bruce has a friend he'll let you go.'

Bruce made no objection. Edith regarded it as a treat to go out with her mother-in-law. The only person who seemed to dislike the arrangement was Mr Raggett. When he found he was to be left alone with Bruce, he seemed on the point of bursting into tears.

The wedding

THE wedding was over. Flowers, favours, fuss and fluster, incense, 'The Voice that breathed o'er Eden,' suppressed nervous excitement, maddening delay, shuffling and whispers, acute long-drawn-out boredom of the men, sentimental interest of the women, tears of emotion from dressmakers in the background, disgusted resignation on the part of people who wanted to be at Kempton (and couldn't hear results as soon as they wished), envy and jealousy, admiration for the bride, and uncontrollable smiles of pitying contempt for the bridegroom. How is it that the bridegroom, who is, after all, practically the hero of the scene, should always be on that day, just when he is the man of the moment, so hugely, pitiably ridiculous?

Nevertheless, he was envied. It was said on all sides that Hyacinth looked beautiful, though old-fashioned people thought she was too self-possessed, and her smile too intelligent, and others complained that she was too ideal a bride - too much like a portrait by Reynolds and not enough like a fashion-plate in the *Lady's Pictorial*.

CHAPTER TWENTY-FOUR

Sir Charles had given her away with his impassive air of almost absurd distinction. It had been a gathering of quite unusual good looks, for Hyacinth had always chosen her friends almost unconsciously with a view to decorative effect, and there was great variety of attraction. There were brides-maids in blue, choristers in red, tall women with flowery hats, young men in tight frock-coats and buttonholes, fresh 'flappers' in plaits, beauties of the future, and fascinating, battered creatures in Paquin dresses, beauties of the past.

As to Lady Cannon, she had been divided between her desire for the dramatic importance of appearing in the fairly good part of the Mother of the Bride, and a natural, but more frivolous wish to recall to the memory of so distin-guished a company her success as a professional beauty of the 'eighties, a success that clung to her with the faded poet-ical perfume of pot-pourri, half forgotten.

Old joys, old triumphs ('Who is she?' from the then Prince of Wales at the opera, with the royal scrutiny through the opera-glass), and old sentiments awoke in Lady Cannon with Mendelssohn's Wedding March, and, certainly, she was more preoccupied with her mauve toque and her embroidered vel-vet gown than with the bride, or even with her little Ella, who had specially come back from school at Paris for the occasion, who was childishly delighted with her long crook with the floating blue ribbon, and was probably the only person present whose enjoyment was quite fresh and with-out a cloud.

Lady Cannon *was* touched, all the same, and honestly would have cried, but that, simply, her dress was really too tight. It was a pity she had been so obstinate with the dressmaker about her waist for this particular day; an inch more or less would have made so little difference to her appearance before the world, and such an enormous amount to her own comfort. 'You look lovely, Mamma – as though you couldn't breathe!' Ella had said admiringly at the reception.

Indeed, her comparatively quiet and subdued air the whole afternoon, which was put down to the tender affection she felt for her husband's ward, was caused solely and entirely by the cut of her costume.

Obscure relatives, never seen at other times, who had given glass screens painted with storks and water-lilies, or silver hair-brushes or carriage-clocks, turned up, and were pushing at the church and cynical at the reception. Very smart relatives, who had sent umbrella-handles and photograph-frames, were charming, and very anxious to get away; heavy relatives, who had sent cheques, stayed very late, and took it out of everybody in tediousness; the girls were longing for a chance to flirt, which did not come; young men for an opportunity to smoke, which did. Elderly men, their equilibrium a little upset by champagne in the afternoon, fell quite in love with the bride, were humorous and jovial until the entertainment was over, and very snappish to their wives driving home.

Like all weddings it had left the strange feeling of futility, the slight sense of depression that comes to English people who have tried, from their strong sense of tradition, to be festive and sentimental and in high spirits too early in the day. The frame of mind supposed to be appropriate to an afternoon wedding can only be genuinely experienced by an Englishman at two o'clock in the morning. Hence the dreary failure of these exhibitions.

Lord Selsey was present, very suave and cultivated, and critical, and delighted to see his desire realised. Mrs Raymond was not there. Edith looked very pretty, but rather tired.

Bruce had driven her nearly mad with his preparations. He had evidently thought that he would be the observed of all observers and the cynosure of every eye. He was terribly afraid of being too late or too early, and at the last moment, just before starting, thought that he had an Attack of Heart, and nearly decided not to go, but recovered when Archie was found stroking his father's hat the wrong way, apparently under the impression that it was a pet animal of some kind. Bruce had been trying, as his mother called it, for a week, because he thought the note written to thank them for their present had been too casual. Poor Edith had gone through a great deal on the subject of the present, for Bruce was divided by so many sentiments on the subject. He hated spending much money, which indeed he couldn't afford, and yet he was most anxious for their gift to stand out among the others and make a sensation.

He was determined above all things to be original in his choice, and after agonies of indecision on the subject of fish-knives and Standard lamps, he suddenly decided on a complete set of Dickens. But as soon as he had ordered it, it seemed to him pitiably flat, and he countermanded it. Then they spent weary hours at Liberty's, and other places of the kind, when Bruce declared he felt a nervous break-down coming on, and left it to Edith, who sent a fan.

When Hyacinth was dressed and ready to start she asked for Anne. It was then discovered that Miss Yeo had not been seen at all since early that morning, when she had come to Hyacinth's room, merely nodded and gone out again. It appeared that she had left the house at nine o'clock in her golf-cap and mackintosh, taking the key and a parcel. This had surprised no-one, as it was thought that 'she had gone to get some little thing for Hyacinth before dressing'. She had not been seen since.

Well, it was no use searching! Everyone knew her odd ways. It was evident that she had chosen not to be present. Hyacinth had to go without saying good-bye to her, but she scribbled a note full of affectionate reproaches. She was sorry, but it could not be helped. She was disappointed, but she would see her when she came back. After all, at such a moment, she really couldn't worry about Anne.

And so, pursued by rice and rejoicings – and ridicule from the little boys in the street by the awning – the newly-married couple drove to the station, '*en route*', as the papers said, with delightful vagueness, '*for the Continent*'.

What did they usually talk about when alone?

Cecil wondered.

The only thing he felt clearly, vividly, and definitely was a furious resentment against Lord Selsey.

'Do you love me, Cecil? Will you aways love me? Are you happy?'

Ashamed of his strange, horrible mood of black jealousy, Cecil turned to his wife.

Accounts

'HOW about your play, Bruce? Aren't you going to work at it this evening?'

'Why no; not just at present. I'm not in the mood. You don't understand, Edith. The Artist must work when the inspiration seizes him.'

'Of course, I know all that, Bruce; but it's six months since you had the inspiration.'

'Ah, but it isn't that only; but the trend of public taste is so bad – it gets worse and worse. Good heavens, I can't write down to the level of the vulgar public!'

'But can you write at all?'

'Certainly; certainly I can; but I need encouragement. My kind of talent, Edith, is like a sort of flower – are you listening? – a flower that needs the watering and tending, and that sort of thing, of appreciation. Appreciation! that's what I need – that's all I ask for. Besides, I'm a business man, and unless I have a proper contract with one of the managers – a regular arrangement and agreement about my work being produced at a certain time – and, mind you, with a cast that *I* select – I just shan't do it at all.'

'I see. Have you taken any steps?'

'Of course I've taken steps – at least I've taken stalls at most of the theatres, as you know. There isn't a play going on at this moment that isn't full of faults – faults of the most blatant kind – mistakes that I myself would never have made. To begin with, for instance, take Shakespeare.'

'Shakespeare?'

'Yes. A play like *The Merchant of Venice,* for example. My dear girl, it's only the glamour of the name, believe me! It's a wretched play, improbable, badly constructed, full of padding – good gracious! do you suppose that if *I* had written that play and sent it to Tree, that he would have put it up?'

'I can't suppose it, Bruce.'

'It isn't sense, Edith; it isn't true to life. Why, who ever heard of a case being conducted in any Court of Law as that is? Do you suppose all kinds of people are allowed to stand up and talk just when they like, and say just what they choose – in blank verse, too? Do you think now, if someone brought an action against me and you wanted me to win it, that you and Bennett could calmly walk off to the Law Courts disguised as a barrister and his clerk, and that you could get me off? Do you suppose, even, that you would be let in? People don't walk in calmly saying that they're barristers and do exactly what they please, and talk any nonsense that comes into their head.'

'I know that; but this is poetry, and years and years ago, in Elizabeth's time.'

'Oh, good gracious, Edith, that's no excuse! It isn't sense. Then take a play like *The Merry Widow.* What about that? Do you suppose that if I liked I couldn't do something better than that? Look here, Edith, tell me, what's the point? Why are you so anxious that I should write this play?'

He looked at her narrowly, in his suspicious way.

'First of all, because I think it would amuse you.'

'Amuse me, indeed!'

'And then, far more, because – Bruce, do you remember assuring me that you were going to make £5,000 a year at least?'

'Well, so I shall, so I shall. You must give a fellow time. Rome wasn't built in a day.'

'I know it wasn't, and if it had been it would be no help to me. Will you look at the bills?'

'Oh, confound it!'

'Bruce dear, if you're not going to work at your play tonight, won't you just glance at the accounts?'

'You know perfectly well, Edith, if there's one thing I hate more than another it's glancing at accounts. Besides, what good is it? What earthly use is it?'

'Of course it would be use if you would kindly explain how I'm going to pay them?'

'Why, of course, we'll pay them – gradually.'

'But they're getting bigger gradually.'

'Dear me, Edith, didn't we a year or two ago make a Budget?'

'Didn't we write down exactly how much every single item of our expenditure would be?'

'Yes; I know we did; but – '

'Well, good heavens, what more do you want?'

'Lots more. You made frightful mistakes in the Budget, Bruce; at any rate, it was extraordinarily underestimated.'

'Why, I remember I left a margin for unexpected calls.'

'I know you left a margin, but you left out coals and clothes altogether.'

'Oh, did I?'

'And the margin went in a week, the first week of your holiday. You never counted holidays in the Budget.'

'Oh! I – I – well, I suppose it escaped my recollection.'

'Never mind that. It can't be helped now. You see, Bruce, we simply haven't enough for our expenses.'

'Oh, then what's the use of looking at the accounts?'

'Why, to see where we are. What we've done, and so on. What do you usually do when you receive a bill?'

'I put it in the fire. I don't believe in keeping heaps of useless papers; it's so disorderly. And so I destroy them.'

'That's all very well, but you know you really oughtn't to be in debt. It worries me. All I want you to do,' she continued, 'is just to go through the things with me to see how much we owe, how much we can pay, and how we can manage; and just be a little careful for the next few months.'

'Oh, if that's all you want – well, perhaps you're right, and we'll do it, some time or other; but not tonight.'

'Why not? You have nothing to do!'

'Perhaps not; but I can't be rushed. Of course, I know it's rather hard for you, old girl, being married to a poor man; but you know you *would* do it, and you mustn't reproach me with it now.'

She laughed.

'We're not a bit too hard up to have a very pleasant time, if only you weren't so – ,' then she stopped.

'Go on; say it!' he exclaimed. 'You want to make out I'm extravagant, that's it! I *have* large ideas, I own it; it's difficult for me to be petty about trifles.'

'But, Bruce, I wasn't complaining at all of your large ideas. You hardly ever give me a farthing, and expect me to do marvels on next to nothing. Of course, I know you're not petty about some things.' She stopped again.

'All right then; I'll give up smoking and golfing, and all the little things that make life tolerable to a hard-working man.'

CHAPTER TWENTY-FIVE

'Not at all, dear. Of course not. There's really only one luxury – if you won't think me unkind – that I think, perhaps, you might try to have less of.'

'What is that?'

'Well, dear, couldn't you manage not to be ill quite so often? You see, almost whenever you're bored you have a consultation. The doctors always say you're quite all right; but it does rather – well, run up, and you can't get much fun out of it. Now, don't be angry with me.'

'But, good God, Edith! If I didn't take it in time, you might be left a young widow, alone in the world, with Archie. Penny-wise and pound-foolish to neglect the health of the breadwinner! Do you reproach me because the doctor said I wasn't dangerously ill at the time?'

'Of course not; I'm only too thankful.'

'I'm sure you are really, dear. Now yesterday I felt very odd, very peculiar indeed.'

'Oh, what was it?'

'An indescribable sensation. At first it was a kind of heaviness in my feet, and a light sensation in my head, and a curious kind of emptiness – nervous exhaustion, I suppose.'

'It was just before lunch, no doubt. I daresay it went off. When I have little headache or don't feel quite up to the mark, I don't send for the doctor; I take no notice of it, and it goes away.'

'But you, my dear – you're as strong as a horse. That reminds me, will you fetch me my tonic?'

When she came back, he said –

'Look here, Edith, I'll tell you what you shall do, if you like. You're awfully good, dear, really, to worry about the bills and things, though it's a great nuisance, but I should suggest that you just run through them with my mother. You know how good-natured she is. She'll be flattered at your consulting her, and she'll be able to advise you if you *have* gone too far and got into a little debt. She knows perfectly well it's not the sort of thing *I* can stand. And, of course, if she were to offer to help a little, well! she's my mother, I wouldn't hurt her feelings by refusing for anything in the world, and the mater's awfully fond of you.'

'But, Bruce, I'd much rather – '

'Oh, stop, Edith. I'm sorry to have to say it, but you're becoming shockingly fussy. I never thought you would have grown into a fidgety, worrying person. How bright you used to seem in the old days! And of course the whole thing about the accounts, and so on, *must* have arisen through your want of management. But I won't reproach you, for I believe you mean well. . . . I've got one of my headaches coming on; I hope to goodness I'm not going to have an attack.'

He looked in the glass. 'I'm rather an odd colour, don't you think so?'

'No; I don't think so. It's the pink-shaded light.'

He sighed.

'Ah, suppose you had married a chap like Reeve – rolling in gold! Are he and Hyacinth happy, do you think?'

'I think they seem very happy.'

'We're lunching there on Sunday, aren't we? Don't forget to order me a buttonhole the day before, Edith.'

'I'll remember.'

She looked at her engagement-book.

'It's not next Sunday, Bruce. Next Sunday we're lunching with your people. You'll be sure to come, won't you?'

'Oh, ah, yes! If I'm well enough.'

Confidences

'I KNOW who you are. You're the pretty lady. Mother won't be long. Shall I get you my bear?'

Hyacinth had come to see Edith, and was waiting for her in the little drawing-room of the flat. The neat white room with its miniature overmantel, pink walls, and brass fire-irons like toys, resembled more than ever an elaborate doll's house. The frail white chairs seemed too slender to be sat on. Could one ever write at that diminutive white writing-desk? The flat might have been made, and furnished by Waring, for midgets. Everything was still in fair and dainty repair, except that the ceiling, which was painted in imitation of a blue sky, was beginning to look cloudy. Hyacinth sat on a tiny blue sofa from where she could see her face in the glass. She was even prettier than before her marriage, now three months ago, but when in repose there was a slightly anxious look in her sweet, initiated eyes. She had neither the air of prosaic disillusion nor that of triumphant superiority that one sees in some young brides. She seemed intensely interested in life, but a little less reposeful than formerly.

'Why, Archie! What a big boy you've grown!'

'Shall I bring you my bear?'

'Oh, no; never mind the bear. Stay and talk to me.'

'Yes; but I'd better bring the bear. Mother would want me to amuse you.'

He ran out and returned with his beloved animal, and put it on her lap.

'Father calls him mangy, but he isn't, really. I'm going to cut its hair to make it grow thicker. I can say all the alphabet and lots of poetry. Shall I say my piece? No; I know what I'll do, I'll get you my cards, with E for ephalunt and X for swordfish on, and see if you can guess the animals.'

'That would be fun. I wonder if I shall guess?'

'You mustn't read the names on them, because that wouldn't be fair. You may only look at the pictures. Oh, won't you have tea? Do have tea.'

'I think I'll wait for your mother.'

'Oh, no; have tea now, quick. Then I can take some of your sugar.'

Hyacinth agreed; but scarcely had this point been settled when Edith returned and sent him off.

'Edith,' Hyacinth said, 'do you know I am rather worried about two things? I won't tell you the worst just yet.'

'It's sure to be all your fancy,' said Edith affectionately.

'Well, it isn't my fancy about Anne. Is it not the most extraordinary thing? Since the day of my wedding she's never been seen or heard of. She walked straight out into the street, and London seems to have swallowed her up. She took nothing with her but a large paper parcel, and left all her luggage, and even her dress that I made her get for the wedding was laid out on the bed. What can have become of her? Of course, I know she has plenty of money, and she could easily have bought an entirely new outfit, and gone away - to America or somewhere, under another name without telling anyone. We've inquired of her father, and he knows nothing about her. It really is a mysterious disappearance.'

'I don't feel as if anything had happened to her,' Edith said, after a pause. 'She's odd, and I fancy she hated your marrying, and didn't want to see you again. She'll get over it and come back. Surely if there had been an accident, we should have heard by now. Do you miss her, Hyacinth?'

'Of course I do, in a way. But everything's so different now. It isn't so much my missing her, if I only knew she was all right. There's something so sad about disappearing like that.'

'Well, everything has been done that can be done. It's not the slightest use worrying. I should try and forget about it, if I were you. What's the other trouble?'

Hyacinth hesitated.

'Well, you know how perfect Cecil is to me, and yet there's one thing I don't like. The Selseys have come back, and have asked us there, and Cecil won't go. Isn't it extraordinary? Can he be afraid of meeting her again?'

'Really, Hyacinth, you are fanciful! What now, now that she's his aunt – practically? Can you really still be jealous?'

'Horribly,' said Hyacinth frankly. 'If she married his uncle a hundred times it wouldn't alter the fact that she's the only woman he's ever been madly in love with.'

'Why, he adores you, Hyacinth!'

'I am sure he does, in a way, but only as a wife!'

'Well, good heavens! What else do you want? You're too happy; too lucky; you're inventing things, searching for troubles. Why make yourself wretched about imaginary anxieties?'

'Suppose, dear, that though he's devoted to me, we suit each other perfectly, and so on, yet at the back of his brain there's always a little niche, a little ideal for that other woman just because she never cared for him? I believe there will always be – always.'

'Well, suppose there is; what on earth does it matter? What difference does it make? Why be jealous of a shadow?'

'It's just because it's such a shadow that it's so intangible – so unconquerable. If she had ever returned his affection he might have got tired of her, they might have quarrelled, he might have seen through her – realised her age and all that, and it would have been over – exploded! Instead of this, he became fascinated by her, she refused him; and then, to make it ever so much worse for me, Lord Selsey, whom he's so fond of and thinks such a lot of, goes and puts her upon a pedestal, constantly in sight, yet completely out of reach.'

'You are unreasonable, Hyacinth! Would you prefer a rival of flesh and blood. Don't be so fanciful, dear. It's too foolish. You've got your wish; enjoy it. I consider that you haven't a trouble in the world.'

'Dear Edith,' said Hyacinth, 'have you troubles?'

'Why, of course I have – small ones. Bruce has taken to having a different illness every day. His latest is that he *imagines* he's a *malade imaginaire*!'

'Good gracious, how complicated! What makes him think that?'

'Because he's been going to specialists for everything he could think of, and they all say he's specially well. Still, it's better than if he were really ill, I suppose. Only he's very tormenting, and hardly ever works, and lately he's taken to making jealous scenes.'

'Oh, that must be rather fun. Who is he jealous of?'

'Why, he thinks he's jealous of his friend Raggett – the most impossible, harmless creature in the world; and the funny thing is whenever Bruce is jealous of anyone he keeps on inviting them – won't leave them alone. If I go out when

Raggett appears, he says it's because I'm so deep; and if I stay he finds fault with everything I do. What do you advise me to do, Hyacinth?'

'Why, give him something more genuine to worry about – flirt with a real person. That would do Bruce good, and be a change for you.'

'I would – but I haven't got time! What chance is there for flirting when I have to be always contriving and economising, and every scrap of leisure I must be there or thereabouts in case Bruce has heart disease or some other illness suddenly? When you are living with a strong young man who thinks he's dangerously ill, flirting is not so easy as it sounds. When he isn't here I'm only too glad to rest by playing with Archie.'

'I see. What do you think could cure Bruce of his imaginary maladies?'

'Oh, not having to work, coming into some money. You see, it fills up the time which he can't afford to spend on amusements.'

Edith laughed.

'It's a bore for you. . . . '

'Oh, I don't mind much; but you see we all have our little troubles.'

'Then, how did you say I ought to behave about the Selseys?'

'Don't behave at all. Be perfectly natural, ignore it. By acting as if things were just as you liked, they often become so.'

There was a ring on the telephone.

Edith went into the next room to answer it, and came back to say –

'Bruce has just rung up. He wants to know if Raggett's here. He says he'll be home in half an hour. He doesn't feel up to the mark, and can't stay at the office.'

'Poor little Edith!'

'And don't for goodness sake bother yourself about Cecil. As if there was any man in the world who hadn't liked somebody some time or other!'

Hyacinth laughed, kissed her, and went away.

Miss Wrenner

ONE day Bruce came into the flat much more briskly than usual. There was a certain subdued satisfaction in his air that Edith was glad to see. He sat down, lit a cigarette, and said –

'Edith, you know how strongly I disapprove of the modern fashion of husbands and wives each going their own way – don't you?'

'Where are you thinking of going, dear?'

'Who said I was thinking of going anywhere?'

'No-one. But it's obvious, or you wouldn't have begun like that.'

'Why? What did you think I was going to say next?'

'Of course, you were going to say, after that sentence about *"you know how strongly I disapprove,"* etc., something like, *"But, of course, there are exceptions to every rule, and in this particular instance I really think that I had better,"* and so on. Weren't you?'

'Odd. Very odd you should get it into your head that I should have any idea of leaving you. Is that why you're looking so cheerful – laughing so much?'

'Am I laughing? I thought I was only smiling.'

'I don't think it's a kind thing to smile at the idea of my going away. However, I'm sorry to disappoint you' – Bruce spoke rather bitterly – 'very sorry indeed, for I see what a blow it will be to you. But, as a matter of fact, I had no intention *whatever* of leaving you at all, except, perhaps, for a few hours at a time. However, of course, if you wish it very much I might arrange to make it longer. Or even to remain away altogether, if you prefer it.'

'Oh, Bruce, don't talk such nonsense! You know I wish nothing of the kind. What's this about a few hours at a time?'

'Naturally,' Bruce said, getting up and looking in the glass; 'naturally, when one has an invitation like this – oh, I admit it's a compliment – I quite admit that – one doesn't want to decline it at once without thinking it over. Think how absurd I should appear to a man like that, writing to say that my wife can't possibly spare me for a couple of hours two or three times a week!'

'A man like what? Who is this mysterious man who wants you for two or three hours two or three times a week?'

'My dear, it can't be done without it; and though, of course, it is rather a nuisance, I daresay in a way it won't be bad fun. You shall help me, dear, and I'm sure I shall be able to arrange for you to see the performance. Yes! you've guessed it; I thought you would. I've been asked to play in some amateur theatricals that are being got up by Mitchell of the F O in aid of the 'Society for the Suppression of Numismatics', or something – I can't think why he chose me, of all people!'

'I wonder.'

'I don't see anything to wonder about. Perhaps he thought I'd do it well. Possibly he supposed I had talent. He may have observed, in the course of our acquaintance, that I was threatened with intelligence! Or again, of course, they want for theatricals a fellow of decent appearance.'

'Ah, yes; of course they do.'

'It would be very absurd for the heroine of the play to be madly in love with a chap who turned up looking like God knows what! Not that I mean for a moment to imply that I'm particularly good-looking, Edith – I'm not such a fool as that. But – well, naturally, it's always an advantage in playing the part of a *jeune premier* not to be quite bald and to go in decently at the waist, and to – Fancy, Miss Wrenner didn't know I was a married man!'

'Miss Wrenner! Who's Miss Wrenner?'

'Why she – Don't you know who Miss Wrenner is?'

'No.'

'Oh, Miss Wrenner's that girl who – a friend of the Mitchells; you know.'

'I *don't* know. Miss Wrenner is quite new to me. So are the Mitchells. What is she like?'

'*Like!*' exclaimed Bruce. 'You ask me what she's *like!* Why, she isn't *like* anything. She's just Miss Wrenner – the well-known Miss Wrenner, who's so celebrated as an amateur actress. Why, she was going to play last Christmas at Raynham, only after all the performance never came off.'

'Is Miss Wrenner pretty?'

'Pretty? How do you mean?'

'What colour is her hair?'

'Well, I – I – I didn't notice, particularly.'

'Is she dark or fair? You must know, Bruce!'

'Well, I should say she was a little darker than you – not a great deal. But I'm not quite certain. Just fancy her not thinking I was married!'

'Did you tell her?'

'Tell her! Of course I didn't tell her. Do you suppose a girl like Miss Wrenner's got nothing to do but to listen to my autobiography? Do you imagine she collects marriage certificates? Do you think she makes a hobby of the census?'

'Oh! then you didn't tell her?'

'Yes, I did. Why should I palm myself off as a gay bachelor when I'm nothing of the sort?'

'When did you tell her, Bruce?'

'Why, I haven't told her yet – at least, not personally. What happened really was this: Mitchell said to me, "Miss Wrenner will be surprised to hear you're a married man," or something like that.'

'Where did all this happen?'

'At the office. Where else do I ever see Mitchell?'

'Then does Miss Wrenner come to the office?'

Bruce stared at her in silent pity.

'*Miss Wrenner! At the office!* Why you must be wool-gathering! Women are not allowed at the F O. Surely you know that, dear?'

'Well, then, where *did* you meet Miss Wrenner?'

'Miss Wrenner? Why do you ask?'

'Simply because I want to know.'

'Oh! Good heavens! What does it matter where I met Miss Wrenner?'

'You're right, Bruce; it doesn't really matter a bit. I suppose you've forgotten.'

'No; I haven't forgotten. I suppose I shall meet Miss Wrenner at the first rehearsal next week – at the Mitchells.'

'Was it there you met her before?'

'How could it be? I have never been to the Mitchells.'

'As a matter of fact, you've never seen Miss Wrenner?'

'Did I say I had? I didn't mean to. What I intended to convey was, not that I had seen Miss Wrenner, but that

CHAPTER TWENTY-SEVEN

Mitchell said Miss Wrenner would be surprised to hear I was married.'

'Funny he should say that – very curious it should occur to him to picture Miss Wrenner's astonishment at the marriage of a man she didn't know, and had never seen.'

'No – no – no; that wasn't it, dear; you've got the whole thing wrong – you've got hold of the wrong end of the stick. He – Mitchell, you know – mentioned to me the names of the people who were going to be asked to act, and among them, Miss Wrenner's name cropped up – I think he said Miss Wrenner was going to be asked to play the heroine if they could get her – no – I'm wrong, it was that *she* had *asked* to play the heroine, and that they meant to get out of it if they could. So, *then*, *I* said, wouldn't she be surprised at having to play the principal part with a married man.'

'I see. *You* said it, not Mitchell. Then are you playing the hero?'

'Good gracious! no – of course not. Is it likely that Mitchell, who's mad on acting and is getting up the whole thing himself, is jolly well going to let me play the principal part? Is it human nature? Of course it isn't. You can't expect it. I never said Mitchell was not human – did I?'

'What is your part, dear?'

'They're going to send it to me tomorrow – typewritten. It's not a long part, and not very important, apparently; but Mitchell says there's a lot to be got out of it by a good actor; sometimes one of these comparatively small parts will make the hit of the evening.'

'What sort of part is it?'

'Oh, no particular *sort*. I don't come on until the second act. As I told you, one of the chief points is to have a good appearance – look a gentleman; that sort of thing.'

'Well?'

'I come on in the second act, dressed as a mandarin.'

'A mandarin! Then you play the part of a Chinaman?'

'No, I don't. It's at the ball. In the second act, there's a ball on the stage – for the hero's coming of age – and I have to be a mandarin.'

'Is the ball given at the Chinese Embassy?'

'No; at the hero's country house. Didn't I tell you – it's a fancy ball!'

'Oh, I see! Then I shouldn't have thought it would have mattered so very much about whether you're good-looking or not. And Miss Wrenner – how will she be dressed at the fancy ball?'

'Miss Wrenner? Oh! Didn't I tell you – Miss Wrenner isn't going to act – they've got someone else instead.'

Anne returns

IT was about six o'clock, and Hyacinth was sitting in her boudoir alone. It was a lovely room and she herself looked lovely, but, for a bride of four months, a little discontented. She was wondering why she was not happier. What was this unreasonable misery, this constant care, this anxious jealousy that seemed to poison her very existence? It was as intangible as a shadow, but it was always there. Hyacinth constantly felt that there was something in Cecil that escaped her, something that she missed. And yet he was kind, affectionate, even devoted.

Sometimes when they spent evenings at home together, which were calm and peaceful and should have been happy, the girl would know, with the second-sight of love, that he was thinking about Eugenia. And this phantom, of which she never spoke to him and could not have borne him to know of, tormented her indescribably. It seemed like a spell that she knew not how to break. It was only a thought, yet how much it made her suffer! Giving way for the moment to the useless and futile bitterness of her jealousy, she had leant her head on the cushion of the little sofa where she sat, when, with a sudden sensation that she was no longer alone, she raised it again and looked up.

Standing near the door she saw a tall, thin figure with a rather wooden face and no expression – a queer figure, oddly dressed in a mackintosh and a golf-cap.

'Why do you burn so much electric light?' Anne said dryly, in a reproachful voice, as she turned a button on the wall.

Hyacinth sprang up with a cry of surprise.

Anne hardly looked at her and walked round the room.

'Sit down. I want to look at your new room. Silk walls and Dresden china. I suppose this is what is called gilded luxury. Do you ever see that the servants dust it, or do they do as they like?'

'Anne! How can you? Do you know how anxious we've been about you? Do you know we weren't sure you were not dead?'

'Weren't you? I wasn't very sure myself at one time. I see you took the chances, though, and didn't go into mourning for me. That was sensible.'

'Anne, will you have the ordinary decency to tell me where you've been, after frightening me out of my life?'

'Oh, it wouldn't interest you. I went to several places. I just went away, because at the last minute I felt I couldn't stand the wedding. Besides, you had a honeymoon. I didn't see why I shouldn't. And mine was much jollier – freer, because I was alone. Cheaper, too, thank goodness!'

'What an extraordinary creature you are, Anne! Not caring whether you heard from me, or of me, for four months, and then coolly walking in like this.'

'It was the only way to walk in. I really had meant never to see you again, Hyacinth. You didn't want me. I was only in the way. I was no longer needed, now you've got that young man you were always worrying about. What's his name? Reeve. But I missed you too much. I was too bored without you. I made up my mind to take a back seat, if only I could see you sometimes. I had to come and have news of you. Well, and how do you like him now you've got him? Hardly worth all that bother – was he?'

'I'll tell you, Anne. You are the very person I want. I need you immensely. You're the only creature in the world that could be the slightest help to me.'

'Oh, so there is a crumpled rose-leaf! I told you he was exactly like any other young man.'

'Oh, but he isn't, Anne. Tell me first about you. Where are you – where are you staying?'

'That's my business. I'm staying with some delightful friends. You wouldn't know them – wouldn't want to either.'

'Nonsense! You used to say you had no friends except mine. You must come and stay here. Cecil would be delighted to see you.'

'I daresay – but I'm not coming. I may be a fool, but I'm not stupid enough for that. I should hate it, besides! No; but I'll look in and see you from time to time, and give you a word of advice. You doing housekeeping, indeed!' She laughed as she looked round.

'Who engaged your servants?'

'Why, I did.'

'I suppose you were too sweet and polite to ask for their characters, for fear of hurting their feelings? I suppose you gave them twice as much as they asked? This is the sort of house servants like. Do you allow followers?'

'How should I know? No; I suppose not. Of course, I let them see their friends when they like. Why shouldn't they? They let me see mine.'

'Yes! that's jolly of them – awfully kind. Of course you wouldn't know. And I suppose the young man, Cecil, or whatever you call him, is just as ignorant as you are, and thinks you do it beautifully?'

'My dear Anne, I assure you – '

'I know what you are going to say. You order the dinner. That's nothing; so can anyone. There's nothing clever in ordering! What are you making yourself miserable about? What's the matter?'

'Tell me first where you're staying and what you're doing. I insist on being told at once.'

'I'm staying with charming people. I tell you. At a boarding-house in Bloomsbury. I'm a great favourite there; no – now I come to think of it – I'm hated. But they don't want me to leave them.'

'Now, Anne, why live like that? Even if you wouldn't stay with us, it's ridiculous of you to live in this wretched, uncomfortable way.'

'Not at all. It isn't wretched, and I thoroughly enjoy it. I pay hardly anything, because I help with the housekeeping. Of course it isn't so much fun as it used to be with you. It's a little sordid; it isn't very pretty, but it's interesting. It's not old-fashioned; there's no wax fruit, nor round table in the middle of the room. It's only about twenty-five years out of date. There are Japanese fans and bead curtains. They think the bead curtains – instead of folding-doors – quite smart and Oriental – rather wicked. Oh, and we have musical evenings on Sundays; sometimes we play dumb crambo. Now, tell me about the little rift within the lute.'

'I always told you every little thing, Anne – didn't I?'

Anne turned away her head.

'Who arranges your flowers?'

'I do.'

'Oh, you *do* do something! They look all right, but I did it much better. Oh – by the way – you mustn't think these are the only clothes I've got. I have a very smart tailor-made coat and skirt which I bought at a sale at a little shop in Brixton. I went to Brixton for the season. There's nothing like the suburbs for real style – I mean real, thoroughly English style. And the funny part is that the suburban English dresses all come from Vienna. Isn't it queer?'

'All right, come to see me next time in your Brixton-Viennese costume, and we'll have a long talk. I think you're pleased I've got a little trouble. Aren't you?'

'Oh, no – I don't want you to have trouble. But I should like you to own *he* isn't so wonderful, after all.'

'But I don't own that – not in the least. The thing is, you see' – she waited a minute – 'I believe I'm still jealous of Mrs Raymond.'

'But she isn't Mrs Raymond any more. You surely don't imagine that he flirts with his aunt?'

'Of course not – how absurd you are! That's a ridiculous way to put it. No – he won't even see her.'

'Is that what you complain of?'

'His avoiding her shows he still thinks of her. It's a bad sign – isn't it? What I feel is, that he still puts her on a pedestal.'

'Well, that's all right. Let her stay there. Now, Hyacinth, when people know what they want – really *want* something acutely and definitely – and don't get it, I can pity them. They're frustrated – scored off by fate, as it were; and even if it's good for them, I'm sorry. But when they *have* got what they wanted, and then find fault and are not satisfied, I can't give them any sympathy at all. Who was it said there is no tragedy like not getting your wish – except getting it? You wanted Cecil Reeve. You've got him. How would you have felt if the other woman had got him instead?'

'You're right, Anne – I suppose. And yet – do you think he'll ever quite forget her?'

'Do you think, if you really tried hard, you could manage to find out what your grievance is, Hyacinth?'

'Yes.'

'Well, then, try; and when you've found it, just keep it. Don't part with it. A sentimental grievance is a resource – it's a consolation for all the prosaic miseries of life. Now I must go, or I shall be late for high tea.'

The ingratitude of Mitchell

SINCE Bruce had had the amateur-theatrical trouble, he had forgotten to have any other illness. But he spent many, many half-hours walking up and down in front of the glass rehearsing his part – which consisted of the words, '*Ah, Miss Vavasour, how charming you look – a true Queen of Night! May a humble mandarin petition for a dance?*' He tried this in many different tones; sometimes serious and romantic, sometimes humorous, but in every case he was much pleased with his reading of the part and counted on a brilliant success.

One evening he had come home looking perturbed, and said he thought he had caught a chill. Eucalyptus, quinine, sal-volatile, and clinical thermometers were lavishly applied, and after dinner he said he was better, but did not feel sufficiently up to the mark to go through his part with Edith as usual, and was rather silent during the rest of the evening.

When he came down to breakfast the next morning, Edith said –

'Do you know Anne's come back?'

'Who's Anne?'

'Anne. Hyacinth's companion. Miss Yeo, I mean.'

'Come back from where?'

'Don't you remember about her going away - about her mysterious disappearance?'

'I seem to remember now. I suppose I had more important things to think about.'

'Well, at any rate, she *has* come back - I've just had a letter - Hyacinth wants me to go out with her this afternoon and hear all about it. At four, I can, of course; it's the day you rehearse, isn't it?'

Bruce waited a minute, then said -

'Curious thing, you *can't* get our cook to make a hot omelette! And we've tried her again and again.'

'It *was* a hot omelette, Bruce - very hot - about three-quarters of an hour ago. Shall I order another?'

'No - oh, no - pray don't - not for me. I haven't the time. I've got to work. You have rather a way, Edith, of keeping me talking. You seem to think I've nothing else to do, and it's serious that I should be punctual at the office. By the way - I shouldn't go out with Hyacinth today, if I were you - I'd rather you didn't.'

'Why not, Bruce?'

'Well, I may want you.'

'Then aren't you going to the Mitchells'?'

'The Mitchells'? No - I am certainly not going to the Mitchells' - under the present circumstances.'

He threw down a piece of toast, got up, and stood with his back to the fire.

'How you can expect me to go to the Mitchells' again after their conduct is more than I can understand! Have you no pride, Edith?'

Edith looked bewildered.

'Has anything happened? What have the Mitchells done?' she asked.

'What have they done!' Bruce almost shouted. He then went and shut the door carefully and came back.

'Done! How do you think I've been treated by these Mitchells – by my friend Mitchell – after slaving night and day at their infernal theatricals? I *have* slaved, haven't I, Edith? Worked hard at my part?'

'Indeed you have, dear.'

'Well, you know the last rehearsal? I had got on particularly well. I told you so, didn't I? I played the little part with a certain amount of spirit, I think. I certainly threw a good deal of feeling and suppressed emotion, and also a tinge of humorous irony into my speech to Miss Vavasour. Of course, I know quite well it doesn't seem of any very great importance, but a lot hinges on that speech, and it isn't everyone who could make the very most of it, as I really believe I did. Well, I happened to be pointing out to Mitchell, yesterday at the office, how much I had done for his play, and how much time and so forth I'd given up towards making the thing a success, then, what do you think he turned round and said? Oh, he is a brute!'

'I can't think!'

'He said, "Oh, by the way, Ottley, old chap, I was going to tell you there's been a change in the scheme. We've altered our plans a little, and I really don't think we shall need to trouble you after all. The fact is, I've decided to cut out the fancy ball altogether." And then people talk of gratitude!'

'Oh, dear, Bruce, that does seem a pity!'

'Seems a pity? Is that all you've got to say! It's an outrage – a slight on me. It isn't treating me with proper deference. But it isn't that I care personally, except for the principle of the thing. For my own sake I'm only too pleased – delighted, relieved. It's for *their* sake I'm so sorry.

The whole thing is bound to be a failure now - not a chance of anything else. The fancy ball in the second act and my little scene with Miss Vavasour, especially, was the point of the play. As Mitchell said at first, when he was asking me to play the part, it would have been *the* attraction.'

'But why is he taking out the fancy ball?'

'He says they can't get enough people. Says they won't make fools of themselves and buy fancy dresses just to make one in a crowd and not be noticed - not even recognised. Says the large fancy ball for the coming of age of the hero in his ancestral halls would have consisted of one mandarin, one Queen of the Night, and a chap in a powdered wig. He thinks it wouldn't have been worth it.'

'Well, I am sorry! Still, couldn't you say your part just the same in an ordinary dress?'

'What! "*Ah, Miss Vavasour, how charming you look - a true Queen of Night!*" Why, do you remember the lines, Edith? Don't you recollect how they refer to our costumes? How could I say them if we weren't in fancy dress?'

'Still, if the whole plot hinges on your scene - '

'Well! all I know is, out it goes - and out I go. The second act will be an utter frost now. They're making a terrible mistake, mind you. But that's Mitchell's business, not mine. It's no kind of deprivation to *me* - you know that. What possible gratification can it be for a man like me - a man of the world - to paint my face and put on a ridiculous dress and make a general ass of myself, just to help Mitchell's rotten performance to go off all right!'

'I don't know. I daresay it would have amused you. I'm sorry, anyhow.'

'I'm sorry enough, too - sorry for them. But if you really want to know the root of the matter, I shrewdly suspect it's really jealousy! Yes, jealousy! It's very odd, when people get keen on this sort of thing, how vain they begin to get! Perfectly childish! Yes, he didn't want me to make a hit. Old Mitchell didn't want to be cut out! Natural enough, in a way, when one comes to think it over; but a bit thick when one remembers the hours I've worked for that man – isn't it?'

'What did you say to him, Bruce, when he first told you?'

'Say? Oh, nothing. I took it very coolly – as a man of the world. I merely said, "Well, upon my word, Mitchell, this is pretty rough," or something of that sort. I didn't show I was hurt or offended in any way. I said, of course, it was like his beastly ingratitude – or words to that effect.'

'Oh! Was he angry?'

'Yes. He was very angry – furious.'

'Then you've had a quarrel with Mitchell?'

'Not a quarrel, Edith, because I wouldn't quarrel. I merely rubbed in his ingratitude, and he didn't like it. He said, "Well, let's hope if you're no longer wasting your valuable life on my theatricals you'll now be able to arrive at the office in fairly decent time," or something nasty like that. Disgusting – wasn't it?'

Edith looked at the clock.

'Too bad,' she said. 'Well, you must tell me all about it – a long account of the whole thing – this afternoon. I won't go out. I'll be at home when you come – to hear all about it. And now – '

'But that wasn't nearly all,' continued Bruce, without moving; 'you'd hardly believe it, but Mitchell actually said that he didn't think I had the smallest talent for the stage! He said I made much too much of my part – over-acted – exaggerated! When I made a point of keeping my rendering of the little scene *particularly* restrained! The fact is, Mitchell's a conceited ass. He knows no more of acting than that chair, and he thinks he knows everything.'

'It's fortunate you hadn't ordered your costume.'

'Yes, indeed. As I told him, the whole thing might have cost me a tremendous lot – far more than I could afford – put me to tremendous expense; and all for nothing! But he said no doubt the costumier would take it back. Take it back, indeed! And that if he wouldn't I could send the costume to him – Mitchell – *and* the bill – it would be sure to come in useful some time or other – the costume, I mean. As though I'd dream of letting him pay for it! I told him at once there could be no question of such a thing.'

'Well, there won't, as you haven't ordered it.'

'Now, Edith, let me beg you not to argue. Isn't it bad enough that I'm slighted by my so-called friends, and treated with the basest ingratitude, without being argued with and nagged at in my own home?'

'I didn't know I was arguing. I beg your pardon. You mustn't worry about this, dear. After all, I suppose if they found at the rehearsals that they didn't really *need* a mandarin – I mean, that the fancy-ball scene wasn't necessary – perhaps from their point of view they were right to cut it out. Don't have a lasting feud with Mitchell – isn't he rather an important friend for you – at the office?'

'Edith, Mitchell shall never set foot under my roof – never darken these doors again!'

'I wonder why, when people are angry, they talk about their roofs and doors? If you were pleased with Mitchell again, you wouldn't ask him to set foot under your roof – nor to darken the door. You'd ask him to come and see us. Anyhow, he won't feel it so very much – because he'll not notice it. He's never been here yet.'

'I know; but Mrs Mitchell was going to call. You will be out to her now, remember.'

CHAPTER TWENTY-NINE

'I can safely promise, I think, never to receive her, Bruce.'

'Good heavens!' cried Bruce, looking at the clock. 'Do you know what the time is? I told you so! I knew it! You've made me late at the office!'

Mitchell behaves decently

FOR the last few days Bruce had been greatly depressed, his temper more variable than ever, and he had managed to collect a quite extraordinary number of entirely new imaginary illnesses. He was very capricious about them and never carried one completely through, but abandoned it almost as soon as he had proved to Edith that he really had the symptoms. Until she was convinced he never gave it up; but the moment she appeared suitably anxious about one disease he adopted another. She had no doubt that he would continue to ring the changes on varieties of ill-health until he had to some extent recovered from the black ingratitude, as he considered it, of Mitchell, in (what *he* called) hounding him out of the amateur theatricals, and not letting him play the part of one line at which he had slaved night and day.

One evening he came home in quite a different mood, bright and cheerful. He played with Archie, and looked in the glass a good deal; both of which signs Edith recognised as hopeful.

'How is your temperature tonight, do you think?' she asked tentatively.

'Oh, *I* don't know. I can't worry about that. A rather gratifying thing has happened today, in fact, very gratifying.' He smiled.

'Really? You must tell me about it.'

'However badly a chap behaves – still, when he's really sorry – I mean to say when he climbs down and begs your pardon, positively crawls at your feet, you can't hold out, Edith!'

'Of course not. Then did Mitchell – '

'And when you have known a fellow a good many years, and he has always been fairly decent to you except in the one instance – and when he is in a real difficulty – Oh, hang it! One is glad to do what one can.'

'Do I gather that there has been a touching scene between you and Mitchell at the office?'

He glanced at her suspiciously. 'May I ask if you are laughing?'

'Oh, no, no! I was smiling with pleasure, hoping you had made it up.'

'Well, yes, it may be weak of me, but I couldn't see the poor fellow's scheme absolutely *ruined* without lending a helping hand. I have got my share of proper pride, as you know, Edith, but, after all, one has a heart.'

'What did he do?'

'Do!' exclaimed Bruce triumphantly. 'Do! Only apologised – only begged me to act with them again – only said that the piece was nothing without me, that's all! So I forgave him, and he was jolly grateful, I can tell you.'

'Fancy! Is it the same part?'

'Of course not. Didn't I tell you that the fancy ball in the second act has been cut out, so of course they don't want a mandarin. No; but Frank Luscombe has given up his part – chucked it, and they have asked me to take it.'

'Is it as long as the other one?'

'Longer! I appear twice. Mind you, in a way it's not such an important part as the other would have been; but the play wouldn't hold together without it, and, as Mitchell said, Frank Luscombe is such a conceited chap he thought himself too grand to play a footman. He didn't have the proper artistic feeling for the whole effect; it appears that he was grumbling all the time and at last gave it up. Then it occurred to Mitchell that perhaps I would help him out, and I said I would. It is a bit of a triumph, isn't it, Edith?'

'A great triumph. Then you will be going back to the rehearsals again?'

'Of course I shall; they begin tomorrow. Mitchell thinks that I shall make the hit of the evening. Some of these comparatively unimportant parts, when they are really well played, are more effective than the chief characters. Mitchell says he saw before, by the rehearsals, what a tremendous lot of talent I had. But it isn't merely talent, as he said; what they all noticed was my Personal Magnetism – and I expect that's it. Fancy a man like Mitchell coming cringing to me, after all that has passed between us! Mind you, it's a distinct score, Edith!'

'It is, indeed. If you have not got your part with you, you won't want to work at it tonight. I wonder, as you seem better, whether you would feel up to listening while I tell you something about the accounts?'

'There you are! How like a woman! The very moment I am a bit cheered up and hopeful and feeling a little stronger, you begin worrying me again.'

'Dear Bruce, I wasn't going to worry you. I don't want you to do anything – anything at all but listen, and it really will take hardly any time at all. You remember you said you weren't strong enough to go through them, and suggested

I should show them to your mother? Well, I went today, and I only want to tell you what happened.'

'Awfully good of you. What did she say?'

'She didn't say much, and she thought she could arrange it, but not without speaking to your father.'

'Oh, I say, really? Well, that's all right then. The girl who plays Miss Vavasour is quite as good as any professional actress, you know; in fact, she would have made a fortune on the stage. She's a Miss Flummerfelt. Her father was German by birth. If she weren't a little bit inclined to be fat, she would be wonderfully handsome. I shall have a little scene with her in the third act, at least, not really a scene exactly, but I have to announce her. I open the door and say, "Miss Vavasour!" and then she rushes up to Lady Jenkins, who is sitting on the sofa, and tells her the bracelet has been found, and I shut the door. But there's a great deal, you know, in the tone in which I announce her. I have to do it in an apparently supercilious but really admiring tone, to show that all the servants think Miss Vavasour had taken the bracelet, but that *I* am certain it isn't true. Frank Luscombe, it seems, used to say the words without any expression at all, just "Miss Vavasour!" like that, in an unmeaning sort of way.'

'I see. Your father was at home at the time, so your mother most kindly said she would go in to him at once, and try to get it settled, just to spare you the suspense of waiting for a letter about it. Isn't it sweet and considerate of her?'

'Awfully. In the second act, Lady Jenkins says to me, "Parker, has an emerald snake bracelet with a ruby head been found in any of the rooms?" and I have to say, "I will inquire, my lady." And then I move about the room, putting things in order. She says, "That will do, Parker; you can go."'

'You seem to make yourself rather a nuisance, then; but do listen, Bruce. I waited, feeling most frightfully uncomfortable, and I am afraid there was a fearful row – I felt so sorry for your mother, but you know the way she has of going straight to the point. She really wasn't long, though it *seemed* long. She came back and said – '

'Of course there's one thing Mitchell asked me to do, but I was obliged to refuse. I can't shave off my moustache.'

'Heavens! You aren't going to play the part of a powdered footman with a moustache?'

'Yes, I shall; Mitchell doesn't know it yet, but I mean to. I can carry it off. I can carry off anything.'

'Well, your mother came back and said that your father had given an ultimatum.'

'Is that all he's given?'

'He will put the thing straight on one condition – it seems it is quite an easy condition; he's going to write and tell it you. Your mother says you must agree at once, not argue, and then everything will be all right.'

'Oh, I am glad. It's all through you, Edith. Thanks, awfully. It's really very good of you. You should have seen how pleased Mitchell was when I said I'd do this for him. Simply delighted. Oh, and Mrs Mitchell is going to call on you. I'll find out which day.'

'I suppose I am to be at home to her now? You told me before not to receive her, you know.'

'Well, no; if you could manage it without being rude, I would rather she only left a card. The Mansions look all right from outside, and they are in a decent neighbourhood and all that, but the flat is so *very* small. I hardly like her to see it.'

'Really, Bruce, you are absurd. Does Mitchell suppose that you live in a palace?'

'Not a *palace*, exactly; but I expect I have given him an impression that it is – well – all right.'

'Well, so it is. If you think the flat unworthy to be seen by Mrs Mitchell, why be on visiting terms with her at all? I don't want to be.'

'But, Edith, you can't refuse the advances of a woman like that, the wife of such a friend of mine as Mitchell. He's a most valuable friend – a splendid fellow – a thoroughly good sort. You've no idea how upset he was about our little quarrel the other day. He said he couldn't sleep at night thinking about it; and his wife, too, was fretting dreadfully, making herself quite ill. But now, of course, it is all right.'

'I am not so sure that it is all right; perhaps you will quarrel again on the moustache question.'

'Oh, no, we shan't! There can't be any more choppings and changings. After telling the whole company that we buried the hatchet and that I am going to take Luscombe's part, he wouldn't care to disappoint them all again. They are very keen, too, on pleasing Miss Flummerfelt, and it seems Mitchell thought she would be particularly glad I was going to act with her instead of Luscombe, because, as I say, Luscombe put so little meaning into the words. It never would have got over the footlights. Old Mitchell will be too pleased to get me back to worry about a trifle like that.'

'Well, that's all right. But do you mind writing to your mother tonight, just a line to thank her for being so kind? It was awfully nice of her, you know – she stuck up for you like anything, and put all the little extravagances on to your ill-health; and, you see, she has spared you having a scene with your father – he is just going to write you a nice note.'

'Yes, I understand, you told me before; but I have got to write a letter tonight, a rather important one. I'll write to the mater tomorrow.'

'Oh, Bruce!'

'My dear girl, business first, pleasure after. To write to one's mother is a pleasure. I wonder what the blessed ultimatum is. Look here, Edith, don't take any engagements for the next two or three weeks, will you? I shall want you every evening for rehearsing. I mean to make a good piece of work of this. I think I shall rather surprise Miss Flummerfelt and Mitchell.'

'Very well; but still I think you might write to your mother. Who is the very important business letter to?'

'Why, it's to Clarkson.'

Jane's sister

'I HAVE made up my mind, Charles, never to go and see Hyacinth again!'

'Indeed! What's the matter? What has happened?'

Sir Charles looked up rather wearily from his book and took off his gold-rimmed spectacles.

'Why should I wear myself out giving advice that is never followed?' indignantly said the lady.

'Why, indeed?'

Lady Cannon looked more than ever like a part of her own furniture, being tightly upholstered in velvet and buttons, with a touch of gold round the neck. She was distinctly put out. Her husband glanced at her and then at the door, as she poured out tea with an ominous air.

'You know how gratified I was, how thankful to see no more of that odious Miss Yeo. I always disapproved of her. I felt she had a bad influence – at any rate not a good one – in the household. I was simply delighted to hear that Hyacinth never saw her now. Well, today I called in to give Hyacinth a suggestion about her under-housemaid – I knew she wanted a new one; and Jane has a sister out of a situation who, I felt certain, would be the very person for her; when, who do I find sitting chatting with Hyacinth, and taking the lead in the conversation in the same odious way she always did, but Miss Yeo!'

'Oh, she has come back, has she? Well, I'm glad she's all right. Poor old Anne! How is she looking?'

'Looking!' almost screamed Lady Cannon. 'As if it mattered how she looked! What did she ever look like? She looked the same as ever. Although it's a lovely day, she had on a mackintosh and a golf-cap and dogskin riding-gloves. She was dressed for a country walk in the rain, but hardly suitable for a visit to Hyacinth. However, that is not the point. The point is her extraordinary impertinence and disrespect to *me*. I naturally took scarcely any notice of her presence beyond a slight bow. I made no reference whatever to her sudden disappearance, which, though exceedingly ill-bred and abrupt, I personally happened to be very glad of. I merely said what I had come to say to Hyacinth: that Jane's sister was looking for a situation, and that Hyacinth's was the very one to suit her. Instead of allowing Hyacinth to speak, what does Miss Yeo do but most impertinently snap me up by saying – what do you suppose she asked me, Charles?'

'How on earth could I possibly guess?'

'She asked me, in a hectoring tone, mind, what I knew about Jane's sister! Daring to ask me a thing like that!'

'What did you say?'

'I answered, in a very proper and dignified way, of course, that I personally knew nothing whatever about her, but that I was always glad to get a good place for a relative of any domestic of mine; so Miss Yeo answered that she thought her sister – I mean Jane – having been with me five years was a circumstance not in her favour at all, quite the contrary, and she would strongly advise Hyacinth not to take Jane's sister on so flimsy recommendation. I was thunderstruck. But this is not all. Before I left, Miss Yeo dared to invite me to go to see her and her friends, and even went so far as to say she could get me an invitation to a musical party they are giving in a boarding-house in Bloomsbury! She says they have charming musical evenings every Sunday, and sometimes play dumb crambo! It was really almost pathetic. To ask *me* to play dumb crambo! The woman can have no sense of humour!'

'I'm not so sure of that,' murmured Sir Charles.

'I merely replied that I had a great deal to do, and could make no engagements at present. I did not like to hurt her feelings by pointing out the glaring incongruity of her suggestion, but really I *was* astonished; and when I said this about the engagements, she answered, "Oh well, never mind; no doubt we shall often meet here," almost as if she guessed my strong aversion to seeing her at Hyacinth's house. Then she went away; and I took the opportunity to advise Hyacinth against encouraging her. Hyacinth seemed extremely vexed and did not take my suggestion at all well. So now, if I know I am to run the risk of meeting that person there and, as I say, am to give advice to no purpose, I prefer to keep away altogether.'

'Did you ask Hyacinth how it was Miss Yeo turned up again?'

'I did; and she answered that Anne could not live without her! Did you ever hear of anything so ridiculous in your life?'

'One can understand it,' said Sir Charles.

'I can't. What use can she possibly be to Hyacinth?'

'It isn't only a question of use, I suppose. They've been great friends for years, but as far as that goes, there's not the slightest doubt Anne could be of great use if she chose.

Hyacinth isn't practical, and has never learnt to be, and Anne is.'

'Then you approve?' said Lady Cannon in a low voice of anger; 'you defend my being insulted, contradicted, and – and – asked to play dumb crambo by such a person as Miss Yeo!'

'Oh, no, my dear; of course I don't. But I daresay she didn't mean to be rude; she was always rather eccentric, and she can be very tactful when she likes. She never was in the slightest degree in the way when she was Hyacinth's companion and actually lived with her, so I don't see how she possibly can be now by going to see her occasionally. Really, I rather like Anne Yeo.'

'Oh, you do,' said his wife furiously; 'then I regret to say we differ very radically. It is *most* unnecessary that you should like her at all.'

'No doubt it is unnecessary, but how can it possibly hurt you? When I say I like her, I mean that I have a friendly sort of feeling for her. I think she's a very good sort, that's all.'

'Then perhaps if you were Cecil Reeve you would like her to live in the house altogether?'

'Oh, I don't go so far as that,' said Sir Charles.

'What I *can't* get over,' continued Lady Cannon, who could never forgive the slightest opposition, and was intensely annoyed and surprised at her husband for once being of a different opinion, 'what I *can't* forgive is her astonishing interference on the question of Jane's sister! When I know that it is the very situation to suit the girl! Now, in future, whatever difficulty Hyacinth may be in, I shall never come forward again with *my* help and experience. I wash my hands of it. It was bad enough before; Hyacinth forgot every single thing I told her, but she never contradicted me and seemed grateful for my advice. But now – now that she has that creature to make her believe that my opinions are not worth considering, of course it is all over. I am sorry for Hyacinth, very sorry. By this, by her own folly, she loses a chance that very few young married women have – a chance of getting an under-housemaid, whose sister has been with me for five years! I have no doubt whatever in my own mind that it would have been arranged today, and that I should have brought the good news back to Jane, if it hadn't been for that unpleasant and unnecessary Miss Yeo. Poor thing! It is very hard on her.'

'What extraordinary creatures women are!' said Sir Charles. 'May I ask whom you are pitying now, Anne or Hyacinth?'

'Neither,' said Lady Cannon, with dignity as she left the room. 'I was pitying Jane's sister.'

The drive

FROM time to time invitations had been received from the Selseys, all of which Cecil had asked Hyacinth to refuse on various pretexts. As she was convinced that he intended never to see Lady Selsey again if he could possibly help it, she made no objection, and did not even remark to him that it would look odd.

One afternoon Cecil was in St James's Street when he remembered that there was an exhibition at Carfax's. He strolled in, and was for the moment quite taken by surprise at the evident gaiety of the crowd. It seemed so incongruous to hear laughter at a private view, where it is now usual to behave with the embarrassed and respectful gloom appropriate to a visit of condolence (with the corpse in the next room).

Then he remembered that it was an exhibition of Max Beerbohm's caricatures, and that people's spirits were naturally raised at the sight of the cruel distortions, ridiculous situations, and fantastic misrepresentations of their friends and acquaintances on the walls.

CHAPTER THIRTY-TWO

Cecil was smiling to himself at a charming picture of the Archbishop of Canterbury, when someone touched him on the shoulder.

He turned round. It was Lord Selsey with his wife. He looked suave and debonair as ever, with his touch of attenuated Georgian dandyism. She had not changed, nor had her long brown eyes lost their sly and fascinating twinkle. Evidently Lord Selsey had not been able - if indeed he had tried - to persuade her to take much trouble about her appearance, but he had somehow succeeded in making her carelessness seem picturesque. The long, rather vague cloak that she wore might pass - at any rate, in a picture-gallery - as artistic, and the flat hat with its long brown feather suggested a Rembrandt, and must have been chosen for her against her will, no doubt by her husband. She really looked particularly plain this afternoon, but at the first glance Cecil admired her as much as ever.

'It's most fortunate we've met you. I have to go on somewhere, and you must drive Eugenia home. You must have a lot to talk about,' Lord Selsey said.

Cecil began to make an excuse.

'Oh, you can't refuse! Are you afraid of me? Don't you want to have a talk with your aunt?' said Eugenia.

He had no choice, and ten minutes later found himself driving in a hansom with his old love.

'Well, tell me, Cecil, aren't you happy? Weren't we quite right?'

'Of course,' said he.

'What an absurd boy you are. It's nice to see you again. I feel just like a mother to you. When am I going to see Hyacinth? Why won't you let me be friends with her? I fell in love with her at first sight. I suppose she worships you, eh? And you take it as a matter of course, and give yourself airs. Oh, I know you! I like Ted very much. He's a wonderful man. He knows everything. He's – what's the word – volatile? No, versatile. He's a walking encyclopædia of knowledge. He can write Persian poetry as soon as look at you, and everything he hasn't learnt he knows by instinct. He has the disposition of an angel and the voice of a gazelle. No, wait a minute; do I mean gazelles? Gazelles don't sing, do they? I must mean nightingales. He sings and plays really beautifully. Why didn't you tell me what a rare creature your uncle is? He has the artistic temperament, as they call it – without any of the nasty temper and horrid unpunctuality that goes with it. I really do admire Ted, Cecil. I think he's perfect.'

'That is most satisfactory,' said Cecil.

She burst out laughing.

'Oh, Cecil, you haven't changed a bit! But marvellous and angelic as Ted is, it's a sort of relief in a way to meet an ordinary man. *You* don't know all about everything, do you? If I asked you the most difficult question about art or science or history or metaphysics, or even dress, you wouldn't be able to answer it, would you? Do you always keep your temper? Is your judgement thoroughly sound? Can you talk modern Greek, and Arabian? I think not. You're full of faults, and delightfully ignorant and commonplace. And it's jolly to see you again.'

'Eugenia, you're the same as ever. Don't go home yet. Let's go for a drive.'

'But oughtn't you to go back to your wife? I daresay she's counting the minutes. Nothing could ever grow prosaic to her, not even being married to you.'

'She's gone out somewhere, with Anne Yeo, I think. Do, Eugenia; I shall never ask you again. Just for once, like old times. I couldn't stand the idea of going to see you at Selsey House; it depressed and irritated me. This is different.'

'All right,' said Eugenia. 'Then make the most of it. I shan't do it again.'

'Where shall we drive?'

'I've always wondered what happened at the very end of the Cromwell Road. Let's drive there, and then you can leave me at home. That will be quite a long way. It's rather a mad idea, Cecil, but it's fun. Isn't it just like Ted to ask you to take me home? You see what a darling, clever creature he is. He guessed – he knew we should be a little excited at meeting again. He wanted to get it over by leaving us quite free to talk.'

'I must say I shouldn't have done that in his place,' said Cecil.

'Oh, you! You might have had some cause of jealousy. He never could. But don't think I shall allow any more freaks like this. In a way I'm rather pleased you haven't forgotten me, Cecil.'

'Who could ever forget you? Who could ever get tired of you?'

'You could; and you would have by now, if I had been foolish enough to marry you.'

She seemed to Cecil, as ever, a delightful medley of impulses, whims, and fancies. For him there was always some magic about her; in her pale radiance he still found the old dazzling, unaccountable charm . . .

'Hyacinth, do let us score off Lady Cannon, and get the housemaid without her help.'

'Why, I have, Anne, I advertised all by myself. Several came to see me yesterday.'

'Well, what did you do about it?'

'Nothing particular. Oh yes; I did. I wrote down the address of one or two. Emma Sinfield, Maude Frick, Annie Crutcher, and Mary Garstin. Which shall I have, Anne – which name do you like best?'

'Emma Sinfield, I think, or if she doesn't do, I rather fancy Garstin. Where does Emma live?'

'In the Cromwell Road. We ought to go and ask for her character today.'

'You go, then, and I'll go with you. You won't know what to ask. I'll do it for you.'

'All right. We may as well drive there as anywhere.'

Anne declared the character quite satisfactory, for Emma Sinfield's late employer, although displaying the most acute conscientiousness, could find no fault with her except a vaulting ambition and wild desire to better herself, which is not unknown in other walks of life, and they were driving away in the motor when they came face to face with Cecil and Eugenia in a hansom. He was talking with so much animation that he did not see them. She was looking straight before her.

Hyacinth turned pale as death and seized Anne's hand. Anne said nothing.

The quarrel

'SO that's why he wouldn't take me to see her! He's been meeting her in secret. My instinct was right, but I didn't think he would do that now. Oh, to think he's been deceiving me!'

'But you mustn't be in such a hurry to judge,' protested Anne; 'it may be just some accidental thing. Hyacinth, do take my advice. Don't say anything about it to him, and see if he mentions it. If he doesn't, then you'll have some reason for suspecting him, and we'll see what can be done.'

'He won't mention it – I know he won't. What accident could make them meet in a hansom in the Cromwell Road? It's too cruel! And I thought she was good. I didn't know she'd be so wicked as this. Why, they've only been married a few months. He never loved me; I told you so, Anne. He ought not to have married me. He only did it out of pique. He never cared for anyone but that woman.'

'Is it hopeless to ask you to listen to reason? So far you have no proof of anything of the kind. Certainly not that he cares for her now.'

'Didn't I see his face? I don't think he's ever looked like that at me.'

If Anne had had a momentary feeling of triumph, of that resignation to the troubles of other people that we are all apt to feel when the trouble is caused by one of whom we are jealous, the unworthy sentiment could not last at the sight of her friend's grief.

'This is serious, Hyacinth. And everything depends on your being clever now. I don't believe that she can possibly mean any harm. She never did. Why on earth should she now? And if you remember, she didn't look a bit interested. There must be some simple explanation.'

'And if there isn't?'

'Then a strong line must be taken. He must be got away from her.'

'To think of having to say that! And he says he loves me! On our honeymoon I began to believe it. Since we have been home I told you I had vague fears, but nothing like this. It's an outrage.'

'It isn't necessarily an outrage for your husband to drive his aunt in a hansom.'

'Don't make fun of me, Anne, when you know she was formerly – '

'But she wasn't, my dear. That's just the point. I'm perfectly sure, I *really* believe, that she never regarded him in that way at all. She looks on him as a boy, and quite an ordinary boy.'

'Ah, but he isn't ordinary!'

'Whatever you do, Hyacinth, don't meet him by making a scene. At present he associates you with nothing but gentleness, affection, and pleasure. That is your power over him. It's a power that grows. Don't let him have any painful recollections of you.'

'But the other woman, according to you, never gave him pleasure and gentleness and all that – yet you see he turns to her.'

'That's a different thing. She didn't love him.'

There was a pause.

'And if I find he doesn't mention the meeting, deceives me about it, don't you even advise me to charge him with it then?'

'It is what I should advise, if I wanted you to have a frightful quarrel – perhaps a complete rupture. If you found out he had deceived you, what would you really do?'

Hyacinth stood up.

'I should – no, I couldn't live without him!'

She broke down.

'I give you two minutes by the clock to cry,' said Anne dryly, 'not a second more. If you spoil your eyes and give yourself a frightful headache, what thanks do you suppose you'll get?'

Hyacinth dried her eyes.

'Nothing he says, nothing he tells me, even if he's perfectly open about the drive this afternoon, will ever convince me that he's not in love with her, and that's the awful thing.'

'Even if that were true, it's not incurable. You're his wife. A thousand times prettier – and twenty years younger! The longer he lives with you the more fond he'll grow of you. You are his life – and a very charming life – not exactly a dull duty. She is merely – at the worst – a whim.'

'Horrid creature! I believe she's a witch,' Hyacinth cried.

'Don't let us talk it over any more. Just as if your own instinct won't tell you what to do far better than I ever could! Besides, you understand men; you know how to deal with them by nature – I never could. I see through them too well. I merely wanted to warn you – being myself a cool looker-on – to be prudent, not to say or do anything irrevocable. If you find you can't help making a scene well, make one. It can't do much harm. It's only that making oneself unpleasant is apt to destroy one's influence. Naturally, people won't stand being bullied and interfered with if they can help it. It isn't human nature.'

'No; and it isn't human nature to share the person one loves with anyone else. That I could never do. I shall show him that.'

'The question doesn't arise. I feel certain you're making a mountain out of a molehill, dear. Well – cheer up!'

Anne took her departure.

As Cecil came in, looking, Hyacinth thought, particularly and irritatingly handsome, she felt a fresh attack of acute jealously. And yet, in spite of her anger, her first sensation was a sort of relenting – a wish to let him off, not to entrap him into deceiving her by pretending not to know, not to act a part, but to throw herself into his arms, violently abusing Eugenia, forgiving him, and imploring him vaguely to take her away.

She did not, however, give way to this wild impulse, but behaved precisely as usual; and he, also, showed no difference. He told her about the pictures, and said she must come and see them with him, but he said nothing whatever of having seen Lady Selsey. He was deceiving her, then! How heartless, treacherous, faithless – and horribly handsome and attractive he was! She was wondering how much longer she could keep her anger to herself, when by the last post she received a note. It was from the Selseys, asking her and Cecil to dine with them on an evening near at hand.

Her hand trembled as she passed the letter to Cecil.

'Am I to refuse?' she asked.

CHAPTER THIRTY-THREE

He answered carelessly –

'Oh, no! I suppose we may as well accept.'

The words 'Have you seen her yet?' were on her lips, but she dared not say them. She was afraid he would tell her the truth.

'Have you any objection?' he asked.

She didn't answer, but walked to the door and then turned round and said –

'None whatever – to *your* going. You can go where you please, and do as you like. But I shall certainly not go with you!'

'Hyacinth!'

'You've been deceiving me, Cecil. Don't speak – please don't – because you would lie to me, and I couldn't bear it. I saw you driving with that woman today. I quite understand that you're beginning to think it would be better I should go to her house. No doubt you arranged it with her. But I'm not going to make it so convenient for you as all that!'

'My dear child, stop, listen! – let me explain. We met accidentally at the picture-gallery, and her husband himself asked me to drive her home. I couldn't get out of it.'

'Oh! He asked you to drive her home! You went a long way round, Cecil. The Cromwell Road is scarcely on the way to Regent's Park from St James's Street. Anyhow, you need not have done it. I have felt for some time that you don't really care for me, and I'm not going to play the part of the deceived and ridiculous wife, nor to live an existence of continual wrangling. I'm disappointed, and I must accept the disappointment.'

'My dearest girl, what do you mean?'

'Let us separate!' she answered. 'I will go abroad somewhere with Anne, and you can stay here and go on with your intrigue. I doubt if it will make you very happy in the end – it is too base, under the circumstances. At any rate, you're perfectly free.'

'You are absolutely wrong, Hyacinth. Terribly wrong – utterly mistaken! I swear to you that today is the first time I've seen her since she married. She wants to know you better – to be your friend. That is why she asked us again. She's devoted to her husband. It was a mere chance, our drive today – there's nothing in it. But still, though I'm absolutely innocent, if you *wish* to leave me, I shall not stand in your way. You want to go abroad with Anne Yeo, do you? Upon my word, I believe you prefer her to me!'

'You are grotesque, Cecil. But, at least, I can believe what she says. I know she would not be treacherous to me.'

'I suppose it was she who put this pretty fancy in your head – this nonsense about my imaginary flirtation with – Lady Selsey?'

'Was it Anne who made you drive with Lady Selsey, and not tell me about it? No, I can't believe you – I wish I could. This is all I've seen, so it's all you acknowledge. For a long time I've known that it was she who was between us. You have always cared for her. I suppose you always will. Well, I am not going to fight with her.'

She threw the note on the table.

'You can answer it! Say you'll go, but that I am going away. I shall probably go tomorrow.'

The door closed behind her. Cecil was left alone.

'By Jove!' he said to himself; and then more slowly, 'By – Jove!'

He lighted a cigarette and immediately threw it away. He rang the bell, and when the servant came, said he didn't want anything. He went into the dining-room, poured out some brandy-and-soda. He looked at it and left it untouched. Then, suddenly, he went upstairs. There was an expression on his face of mingled anxiety, slight amusement, and surprise. He went to her room. The door was locked.

'Hyacinth,' he said in a low voice, 'Hyacinth, darling, do open the door.... I want to speak to you. Do answer. You are quite mistaken, you know.... You know I don't care for anyone but you, dear. It's too absurd. Open the door!'

'Please go away, Cecil.'

'But, I say, I *insist* on your opening the door! I *will* come in; you're treating me shamefully, and I won't stand it. Do you hear?'

She came close to the door and said in a low, distinct voice –

'I don't wish to see you, and you must please leave me alone. I'm busy.'

'Busy! Good Lord! What are you doing?'

'I'm packing,' she answered.

He waited a second, and then went downstairs again and sat down in the arm-chair.

'By Jove!' he exclaimed again. 'By – Jove!'

His thoughts were more eloquent. But a baffled Englishman is rarely very articulate.

Anne and Eugenia

'IF you please, my lady, there's someone called to see you.'

Eugenia looked up in surprise. She was in the library, occupied in cataloguing Lord Selsey's books.

'It's a - well - it's not exactly a young person, my lady. She says she's sure you will see her. The name is Miss Yeo.'

'Miss Yeo?' Eugenia looked puzzled. 'Show her in at once.'

Anne came in, coolly.

'I'm afraid you hardly remember me, Lady Selsey,' she said. 'We met last summer. I was Miss Verney's companion.'

Eugenia held out her hand cordially.

'Of course, I remember you very well. Why, it was here we met! At that musical party! Do sit down, Miss Yeo. Won't you take off your mackintosh?'

'No, thanks. I must apologise for intruding. The fact is I've come about something important. It's about Mrs Reeve.'

'Mrs Reeve?' Eugenia leant eagerly forward. 'Do, do tell me! Anything about her interests me so much.'

'You'll think me very impertinent, Lady Selsey. But I can't help it. I'll come straight to the point.'

CHAPTER THIRTY-FOUR

'Do, please.'

'Mrs Reeve has had a terrible quarrel with her husband. She would have left him this morning, but that I persuaded her to wait. I came to tell you because I felt sure you would be sorry. It's about you, Lady Selsey.'

'About me!'

'Yes. She saw you driving with her husband, and he didn't mention it. She's jealous of you. Of course he explained it, but she doesn't believe him. I thought he probably would not say anything about it to you. I know, of course, it's a sort of misunderstanding. But I thought perhaps you could do some-thing about it to make it all right.'

'I *am* grieved,' said Eugenia, clasping her hands. 'You know Cecil was an old friend of mine, don't you? I met him again after many months, and in a foolish impulse we went for a drive. That is all, of course. Miss Yeo, I'm sure you're her true friend. This quarrel must be made up. What can I do? What do you advise?'

'Even if this particular quarrel is patched up, she would always be suspicious and jealous of you. It makes her miserable.'

'Poor darling, how ridiculous! I'm sure I'd be only too pleased never to see the silly boy again.'

'I quite understand all that, but, you see, she's very proud. That sort of rupture – all being connected as you are – would be noticeable to other people, and she's very sensitive – she couldn't stand it.'

Eugenia thought a moment.

'Suppose we went away somewhere for a year? That would give her time to forget this nonsense. My husband has been trying to persuade me to go to the Ionian Islands with him – yachting. He'll be only too pleased if I say I will. I'm a wretched sailor, but if it would do any good – '

'It would be perfect. It would all come right.'

'Then I'll do it. I had asked them to dinner for next week. I haven't had an answer yet. I'll telegraph, putting them off, and explaining why.'

'That would be splendid,' said Anne.

'Then it's settled,' answered Eugenia briefly.

Anne got up.

'Of course it must be understood that you know nothing about it – I mean about the quarrel,' she said.

'Of course not. Not a soul, not my husband, nor Cecil, nor his wife shall ever know a word about your visit, Miss Yeo.'

'That is very kind of you, Lady Selsey. I – well, you know I'm devoted to Hyacinth. At first I was almost selfishly glad about this. I could have got her back. We could have gone away together. But I can't see her miserable. She has such a mania for Cecil Reeve! Isn't it extraordinary?'

'Most extraordinary,' replied Eugenia emphatically.

'And since she's got him, she may as well be happy with him,' Anne added.

'Of course. And she will. This misunderstanding won't do any harm in the long run,' said Eugenia. 'If he had any real fear of losing her, it would do him a great deal of good. He's devoted to her really, more than either of them knows.'

'I daresay,' said Anne dryly. 'It's sure to be fixed up soon, and then I'm going away too.'

'You are! Why, Miss Yeo?'

'Oh, I don't know. I feel I'm not in the picture. I hate the sight of turtle-doves. If I've been able to do her a good turn in this little trouble, it will be a great consolation where I'm going.'

'I'm afraid you're not happy, Miss Yeo?' said Eugenia impulsively.

'I don't know that I am, particularly. But does it matter? We can't all be happy.'

'I'm sorry. I want everyone to be happy.'

'I suppose it's always a mistake to make an idol of any-one,' said Anne. 'I'm afraid Hyacinth thinks that is what her husband has done about you.'

'*That* would indeed be inexcusable!'

'She thought that the hopelessness of it had made him idealise you, and even that worried her; but when she saw you together, and it seemed – well, concrete treachery – she was furious.'

'It will bring them nearer than they have ever been before,' assured Eugenia.

'Good-bye,' said Anne. 'I'll write to you – once – and tell you what has happened.'

'Do, and be quick; I shall be busy buying yachting dresses. By the way, you might take the telegram.'

Anne waited while she wrote –

'Frightfully sorry, dinner next week unavoidably post-poned as unexpectedly leaving town for season. Writing. Eugenia Selsey.'

'I will write to her when I've arranged it with my husband.'

Anne took the telegram.

'That woman'

BY the end of their drive Eugenia had quite come to the conclusion that Cecil was as foolish as ever, and that she would not be alone with him again. At first it had amused her to see him once more, but when she saw the infatuation revive, she was bored and sorry – and particularly sorry she had given him the opportunity of expressing it. She had told him, definitely, that she would not see him again except with Hyacinth. He had declared it was merely the excitement of having met her, and implored forgiveness, undertaking in future to regard her as a friend merely.

This reconciliation – for they had had quite a quarrel in the cab coming back – and the solemn compact and promise on Cecil's part to ignore the old terms, had led to the invitation that Hyacinth regarded as an insult added to injury.

Cecil's conscience, then, as he sat by the fire that night pricked him not at all, for had he not made the best of resolutions? Indeed, privately, he rather plumed himself on his honourable conduct, forgetting perhaps that it was inspired more by Eugenia's attitude than by his own inclination.

Probably he hardly realised that, had Eugenia used her influence differently, there was hardly anything he would not have done. To him facts were everything – and he believed he had meant no harm.

He was still, he knew, to a great extent under the charm of his old friend. Still, that did not seem to have anything to do with his love for Hyacinth. He did not believe her threat of leaving him, but the mere picture of such a thing gave him great pain. He thought that if he had not been exactly in love with her when they married he was now; and could not at all imagine himself living without her. What, then, did he really want? He did not formulate it.

Au fond, he was more flattered than annoyed at the position Hyacinth took up. He was amused, positively impressed, at her spirit. Had she not been so excessively pretty, it would have made him more angry and more anxious to rebel at the idea of her dictation. Perhaps his happiness with Hyacinth had gone almost too smoothly. He had become quite spoilt by her exquisite responsiveness, too much accustomed to the delightful homage of her being so much in love with him, to her charm in every way. He didn't at all fancy the idea of the smallest amount of this tribute being diminished. Suppose he offered never to see Eugenia again? After all, he had avoided her until today. He could continue to do so. But he had just arranged with her that they should all be friends. It would seem ridiculous. Besides, he *wanted* to see her!

Oh! what an infernal nuisance the whole thing was! It was such an awkward situation. As the thought developed, gradually, that he really would have to choose, there could be no sort of doubt that he would choose Hyacinth. . . .Yes, his fancy for Eugenia was the shadow, a will-o'-the-wisp; Hyacinth was the reality – a very lovely and loving reality.

Hers was the insidious charm that grows rather than dazzles, the attraction that increases with time. He could not imagine, however long they might be married, her becoming ever a comrade merely. Mentally and physically, she held him far more since their marriage than before; he had found in her a thousand delightful qualities of which he had never dreamed.

Then that mad, capricious creature, Eugenia, meeting him, must make him take her for a drive and spoil it all! He began to get rather angry with her. Certainly since this row about her, he felt he liked her less. Why couldn't she stick to Uncle Ted - as she thought him so marvellous - and leave *him* alone?

With this unjust and inconsistent movement of irritation, he again attempted speaking to Hyacinth through the door, assuring her that if she would only open it, he would convince her. But as he received no answer, he was too proud to say any more, and retired sulkily to his own room.

To his great surprise, he fell asleep almost immediately.

The next morning he went out without seeing Hyacinth, but left a message that he would be in at one, and wished to speak to her. He thought this would give her time to recover, or even perhaps to speak to Anne. At heart he did not believe Anne would give her any but sensible advice, though he now began to feel a little jealous of her influence.

When he came back he found Hyacinth in the boudoir. She looked pale, but particularly pretty, with a little air of tragic composure.

'May I ask if you still think seriously of leaving me?' he asked sarcastically.

CHAPTER THIRTY-FIVE

'I haven't settled anything yet.'

'Why is that? Won't Anne go with you?'

She avoided answering, but said, 'I've been thinking things over, Cecil, and assuming that what you told me yesterday was true – that you met *that woman* for the first time again yesterday – I will not – go away. We will remain outwardly as we have been. But as long as I believe, as I do, that you are in love with her, I intend to be merely a friend to you.'

'A friend? What utter nonsense! I refuse to consent to anything so absurd. I won't stand it!'

'I shall not,' continued Hyacinth, taking no notice, 'interfere with your freedom at all. I don't ask you not to see her. You can go there when you like. I couldn't bear the idea that I was putting a restraint on your liberty, so that even if you offered – which you haven't – to give up seeing her at all – I wouldn't accept such a *sacrifice!*'

Cecil laughed impatiently.

'Considering I've avoided her till yesterday – '

'Ah, you admit it! That shows – that proves you care for her.'

'Don't you own yourself you were probably wrong – that you misunderstood about the drive?' he asked.

'I assume that I can believe your word – that is why I'm not leaving you. Do you accept my terms?'

His eyes flashed; he walked towards her violently, overturning a little table.

'No, I don't,' he said, 'and I never shall! It's infernal, unjust, ridiculous. You are my wife!'

She seemed not offended at his violence, but she said –

'Think it over till tomorrow. You understand that unless you agree to our each going our own way I shall not remain here.'

He came a step nearer. At this moment the door opened and the servant announced lunch.

Cecil, without saying another word, went out of the house. The door banged loudly.

At the sound Hyacinth burst into tears. 'Oh, why am I so miserable?' she sobbed.

Raggett's sense of humour

'EDITH,' said Bruce, 'I'm rather worried about Raggett.'

'Are you? Why?'

'Well, the last time I met him, he came up and asked me if I knew the difference between a sardine and a hedgehog. Of course I said no, thinking it was some riddle, but he only answered, "Then you *must* be a fool!"'

Edith smiled.

'Is that all?'

'No, it is *not* all. It will give you a shock, what I'm going to tell you now. At the office – at the *office*, mind – I received a letter from Raggett, written on a crumpet.'

'On a what?'

'On a crumpet. The letter was gummed on; the thing had a stamp, and was properly addressed to me, and it came through the post. The note itself was quite rational, but the postscript – what do you suppose the postscript said?'

'I can't think.'

'It said, "P S – Please excuse my writing to you on a crumpet, as I haven't a muffin!"'

Edith laughed.

'It's all very well to laugh, but it's a very sad thing. The poor chap is going off his head. I don't know what to do about it.'

'He isn't really, Bruce. I know what it is. I can explain the whole thing. Last time I saw him – he called the day you were rehearsing – he said he had given up being a Legitimist, and was going to try, if possible, to develop a sense of humour. He thinks for one thing it will please *me*. I'm sure he hopes you will tell me the story about the crumpet, and that I shall admire him for it.'

'Do you seriously mean that he's trying to be funny on your account?'

'That's the idea.'

'But what have you to do with his career? What is it to you? I mean, what is it to him – whether you like people to be funny or serious?'

'Nothing, really.'

'You admit openly, Edith, that you know he has such a liking for you that he is becoming a clown in the hope that you will think him witty?'

'That is it. He's afraid he's a bore – too dull. He wants to amuse me. That's all.'

'What right has he to wish anything of the kind? Have you not got me, if you wish to be amused? If I thought that you were right – but, mind you, I don't; all women have their little vanities, and I believe it's a delusion of yours about Raggett – I think he's simply been getting a little queer in the head lately. However, if I did think it, I should consider it an outrage. To write me a letter on a crumpet, as a *joke*! Joke, indeed! Men have been called out for less, Edith.'

Bruce thought a little while, then he said –

'I'll take no notice of it this time. But if I have any more nonsense from Raggett, I shall ask for an explanation. I shall say to him, "My wife tells me that your tone, which I consider greatly wanting in deference to me, is meant as homage to her! What do you mean?" I shall say to Raggett, just like this, "What the – "'

Edith already regretted her candour. 'No, no; you mustn't bully poor Raggett. Perhaps I was wrong. I daresay he wanted to amuse us both.'

'That is more likely,' said Bruce, relenting. 'But he's going the wrong way to work if he wishes to retain my good opinion of him. And so I shall tell him if he gives me any more of this sort of thing.'

'Instead of bothering about Raggett, I do wish you would answer your father's letter, Bruce.'

'Good gracious; surely I need not answer it at once!'

'I think you should.'

'Well, what does he say?'

Bruce had such a dislike to plain facts that he never, if he could avoid it, would read a letter to himself containing any business details.

Edith took out the letter.

'Why I've told you already, but you wouldn't listen. On condition that you are not late at the office or absent from it except on holidays, for any reason, either pleasure or illness, for the next two years, your father will pay the debt and help you to start fresh.'

'But how can I be sure I shan't be ill? A man in my delicate state.'

'Oh, assume that you won't. Try not to be – promise to be well. Surely it's worth it?'

'Very well, perhaps it is. What a curious, eccentric man the governor is! No other man would make such extraordinary conditions. Look here, you can write for me, Edith dear, and say I accept the arrangement, and I'm awfully obliged and grateful and all that. You'll know how to put it. It's a great nuisance though, for I was thinking of giving up the whole of tomorrow to rehearsing – and chucking the office. And now I can't. It's very awkward.'

'Well, I'll write for you, though you certainly ought to do it yourself, but I shall say you are going to see them, and you will – next Sunday, won't you?'

'Sunday would be rather an awkward day. I've made a sort of vague engagement. However, if you insist, very well.'

'I can't quite understand,' said Edith, after a pause, 'how it is that the rehearsals take so long now. Yesterday you said you had to begin at eleven and it wasn't over till half-past four. And yet you have only two or three words to say in the second act and to announce someone in the first.'

'Ah, you don't understand, my dear. One has to be there the whole time so as to get into the spirit of the thing. Rehearsals sometimes take half the night; especially when you're getting to the end. You just stop for a minute or two for a little food, and then start again. Yesterday, for instance, it was just like that.'

'Where did you lunch?'

'Oh, I and one or two of the other men looked in at the Carlton.'

'It can't have taken a minute or two. It's a good distance from Victoria Street.'

'I know, but we went in the Mitchells' motor. It took no time. And then we rushed back, and went on rehearsing. *How* we work!'

'And what were you going to do tomorrow?'

He hesitated. 'Oh, tomorrow? Well, now, after this promise to the governor, I shan't be able to get there till half-past four. I should have liked to get there by twelve. And it's very awkward indeed, because Miss Flummerfelt asked me to take her out to lunch, and I half promised. In fact, I could hardly get out of it.'

'She asked you to take her alone?'

'Oh, in a thing like this you all become such pals and comrades; you don't stop to think about chaperones and things. Besides, of course, I meant to ask you to join us.'

'Very sweet of you.'

'There's the post,' remarked Bruce.

He went out into the little hall. Edith went with him.

'Who is your letter from?' asked Edith, as they went back. Bruce blushed a little.

'It *looks* something like Miss Flummerfelt's handwriting.'

'Oh, do show me the letter!' said Edith, as he seemed about, having read it, to put it in the fire. He was obliged to allow her to take it, and she read –

DEAR MR OTTLEY,

It's very kind of you to ask me to lunch tomorrow, but I can't possibly manage it. I'm engaged tomorrow, besides which I never go out anywhere without my mother.

Yours sincerely,

ELSA FLUMMERFELT.

Edith smiled. 'That's fortunate,' she said. 'After all, you won't have the awkwardness of putting her off. What a good thing.'

'I assure you, Edith,' said Bruce, looking very uncomfortable, 'that I had forgotten which way it was. But, of course, I felt I ought – as a matter of decent civility to Mitchell, don't you know – to ask her once. I suppose now that you won't like me going to the rehearsals any more?'

'Oh, no! not at all,' said Edith serenely. 'I see, on the contrary, that there is nothing at all to be alarmed at. What a nice girl Miss Flummerfelt must be! I like her handwriting.'

'I see nothing particularly nice about her.'

'But she's wonderfully handsome, isn't she?'

'Why no; she has a clumsy figure, drab hair, and a colourless complexion. Not at all the type that I admire.'

'You told me the other day that she was an ideal blonde. But, of course, that,' said Edith, 'was before she refused to lunch with you!'

Sir Charles

EARLY that afternoon Hyacinth was sitting in the library in the depths of depression when Sir Charles Cannon was announced. She had forgotten to say she was not at home, or she would not have received him; but it was now too late.

He came in, and affecting not to see there was anything the matter, he said –

'I've come for some consolation, Hyacinth.'

'Consolation? Is Aunt Janet in a bad temper? I saw her pass yesterday in a green bonnet. I was afraid there was something wrong.'

'Is that so? This is interesting. Can you actually tell the shade of her temper from the shade of her clothes?'

'Yes. Can't you?'

'I don't know that I ever thought of it.'

'When Auntie is amiable she wears crimson or violet. When she's cross she always introduces green or brown into the scheme. You watch her and you'll find I'm right.'

'I have observed,' said Sir Charles slowly, 'that when we're going out somewhere that she isn't very keen about she always wears a good deal of shiny jet, and when we're at

home alone and something has happened to vex her I seem
to remember that she puts on a certain shaded silk dress that
I particularly hate – because you never know where you are
with it, sometimes it's brown and sometimes it's yellow.
It depends on the light, and anyhow it's hideous; it's very
stiff, and rustles.'

'I know. Shot taffeta! Oh, that's a *very* bad sign. Has she
worn it lately?'

'Yes, she has, a good deal.'

'What's been the matter?'

'Oh, she has – may I smoke? Thanks – some mysterious
grievance against you. She's simply furious. It seems it has
something to do with somebody called Jane's sister.'

'Oh! Tell me about it.'

'Well, it appears Jane's sister wants to come and be your
housemaid, and you won't let her, and she's very disappointed. You've no idea how badly you've behaved to Jane's
sister.'

'Fancy! How horrid of me! Tell me some more.'

'And it's all through Miss Yeo. In fact, Anne's enmity to
Jane's sister is quite extraordinary – unheard of. By some
deep and malicious plot it seems she prevented you yield-
ing to your better nature – or something – and there it is.
Oh, Hyacinth, I wish she hadn't! It makes your aunt so
nasty to me. Yes, *I* get the worst of it, I can tell you.'

'Poor Charles! I am sorry. If I'd known that you were
going to suffer for it. I should have insisted on engaging
her. Is it too late now? I believe we've got another housemaid, but can't she come too?'

'I fear it is too late. And when Janet has got accustomed to
a grievance she doesn't like having it taken away either. No,
nothing can be done. And I *am* having a time of it! However,
it's a great comfort to see you. You're never worried are you?'

'Never worried! Why, Charles, if you only knew – of course I've *been* divinely happy, but just now I'm in real trouble.'

He looked at her.

'But I can't bear anyone to know it.'

'Then don't tell me,' he said.

'Oh, I must tell you! Besides, very likely you'll hear it soon.' Then she added, 'It's not impossible that Cecil and I may separate.'

'My dear child!'

'I believe he likes someone else better.'

'This is nonsense, Hyacinth. A mere lovers' quarrel. Of course, you must make it up at once. He's devoted to you. Who could help it?'

She broke down.

'Oh, Charles, I'm so unhappy.'

Sir Charles felt furious indignation at the idea that any man could cause those tears to flow. He put his arm round her as if she had been a child.

'My dear Hyacinth, don't be foolish. This is not serious; it can't be.' He had known her intimately since she was ten and had never seen her cry before.

The old tenderness surged up in his heart.

'Can I do anything, dear?'

'No, no, Charles. I should *die* if he knew I had told you!'

'Surely it must be your imagination.'

'I think he deceives me, and I know he prefers that horrid woman.'

'Don't cry, Hyacinth.'

She cried more, with her face buried in a cushion.

He kissed the top of her head pityingly, as if in absence of mind. He remembered it was the first time for eight years. Then he got up and looked out of the window.

'Cecil can't be such a blackguard. He's a very good fellow. Who is this new friend that you're making yourself miserable about?'

'It isn't a new friend; it's Lady Selsey.'

Sir Charles stared in amazement.

'Eugenia! Why she's the best creature in the world – utterly incapable of – I'm perfectly certain she cares for nobody in the world but Selsey. Besides, to regard her as a rival of yours at all is grotesque, child.'

'Ah, yes; you say that because you regard me almost as your daughter, and you think I'm pretty and younger, and so on. But that's not everything. There are no standards, no rules in these things. And even if there were, the point is not what she is, but what he thinks her. He thinks her wonderful.'

'Well, what has happened?'

'Never mind the details. I know his *feelings* – and that is everything.'

'You've had a quarrel, I suppose, and he's gone out of the house in a temper. Is that it?'

'I told him that I should leave him and go away somewhere with Anne.'

'Anne wouldn't go, of course.'

'You're right. She wouldn't when I asked her this morning, or I should be on my way to Paris by now.'

'If he treated you really badly,' said Sir Charles, 'she would have gone. It must be that she knows there's nothing in it.'

'I've offered to remain, on condition that we are merely friends. And he won't hear of it.'

'No wonder,' said Sir Charles. 'Now Hyacinth you know you've always been a spoilt child and had everything on earth you wanted. You must remember in life sometimes little things won't go right.'

'Anything might have gone wrong – anything in the world, and I would have borne it and not cared – but *that*!'

'I would do anything to see you happy again,' he said. 'You know that.'

She looked up. There is a tone in the accents of genuine love that nothing can simulate. She was touched.

'Look here, Hyacinth, promise me to do nothing without letting me know.'

'I promise, Charles.'

'And I assure you that everything will come right. I know – I've had a little experience of the world. Won't you trust my judgement?'

'I'll try. You are a comfort, Charles.'

'And to think that I came to you for consolation!' he said. 'Well, Hyacinth, I shall bury this – forget all about it. Next time I see you you'll be beaming again. It's a passing cloud. Now, what do you think *I*'ve got to do? I've got to go home and fetch Janet to go to a meeting of the Dante Society at Broadwater House.'

'Good gracious! What on earth does Aunt Janet know about Dante?'

'Nothing, indeed. I believe she thinks he wrote a poem called "Petrarch and Laura". But someone told her it's the right thing to do; and when Janet thinks anything is the right thing – !' He took his hat and stick. 'Try and forgive Cecil. I'm sure he adores you. We all do.'

'Thanks, Charles. And I do hope Aunt Janet won't be wearing her green bonnet this afternoon.'

'Thank you, dear, I trust not. Good-bye.'

Rehearsing

'HOW did you get on at the rehearsal today?' Edith asked.

Bruce was looking rather depressed. 'Not very well. You can't think how much jealousy there is in these things! When you rehearse with people day after day you begin to find out what their real characters are. And Mitchell always had a very nasty temper. Of course, *he* says it's quick and soon over. He thinks that's the best kind to have. I think he's rather proud of it. The fact is he has it so often that it's as bad as if it were slow and *not* soon over. First of all, you know, there was a kind of scene about whether or not I should shave for the part of the footman. *He* said I ought. *I* declared I wouldn't ruin my appearance just for the sake of a miserable little part like that; in fact, I might say for a few minutes in a couple of hours during one evening in my life! At last we compromised. I'm to wear a kind of thing invented by Clarkson, or somebody like that, which gums down the moustache, so that you don't notice it.'

'But you don't notice it, anyhow, much.'

'What do you mean by that?'

216

CHAPTER THIRTY-EIGHT

'I don't mean anything. But I never heard of anybody noticing it. No-one has ever made any remark to me about it.'

'They wouldn't take the liberty. It can't have passed *un*noticed, because, if it had, why should Mitchell ask me to shave?'

'There is something in that, I must admit,' she answered.

'Well, I consented to this suggestion of Mitchell's, though I don't like it at all, and I daresay it will spoil my appearance altogether. It was about something else we had a bit of a tiff this afternoon. We were going through the whole play, and one or two people were to be allowed to see us. Mitchell said he expected a certain manager, who is a pal of his, to criticise us – give us some hints, and so on. I saw a man who hadn't been there before, and I spotted him at once. He looked like a celebrity. Without waiting for an introduction, I went up and asked him what he thought of our performance. He said it seemed all right. Then I asked him if he considered my reading of my part what he would have done himself, and he laughed and said, "Yes, very much the same." We were criticising the other actors and having a long talk – at least *I* was having a long talk – *he* didn't say much – when he suddenly said, "I'm afraid you must excuse me," and went away. Then Mitchell came up to me and said, "How on earth is it you had so much to say to that chap?" I said (still believing he was the manager) that he was an old acquaintance of mine, at least, I had known him a long time – on and off – and that he seemed very pleased to see me again. Mitchell said, "Oh, you met him before today, did you?" I answered, "Yes, rather," and I said, "He was very friendly, I must say. He's very pleased with my performance. I shouldn't be surprised if he sends me a box for his First Night. If he does you must come, you and Mrs Mitchell." As a matter of fact, I *had* hinted that I should like a box for the First Night at the Haymarket, and he had laughed good-naturedly, and said, "Oh, yes." So it was really no wonder that I regarded that as a promise. Well, when I told him that, Mitchell said, "He offered you a box, did he? Very nice of him. You know who he is, don't you? He's a man who has come to see about the electric lighting for the footlights. *I*'ve never seen him before." Now, you know, Edith, it was a most infernal shame of Mitchell to let me make the mistake with his eyes open. Here was I talking about acting and plays, deferentially consulting him, asking for artistic hints and boxes from an electrical engineer! Oh, it's too bad, it really is.'

'So you quarrelled with Mitchell again?'

'We had a few words.'

'Then the manager was not there?'

'No; he'd promised, but didn't turn up. I told Mitchell what I thought of him in very plain terms. I went so far even as to threaten to throw up my part, and he said, "Well, all right, if you don't like it you can give it up at any time," I said, "Who else could you get at the last minute to play a footman's part?" and he said, "Our footman!"'

'That would be realism, wouldn't it?'

'I was awfully hurt, but it was settled I was to stick to it. Then there are other things. That horrid Miss Flummerfelt – how I do dislike that girl – had been silly enough to go boasting to Mrs Mitchell of my invitation to lunch the other day.'

'Boasting!' said Edith.

'Yes, it was a shame, because of course I only asked her simply and solely as a way of returning some of the Mitchells' hospitality – '

'Then why did you mind their knowing?' Edith inquired.

'I *didn't* mind their knowing. How stupid you are, Edith. But I objected strongly to the tone in which Miss Flummerfelt had evidently spoken of it – to the light in which she had represented the whole thing. Mrs Mitchell came up to me in her soft purring way – what a horrid little woman she is!'

'Why, you told me she was so sweet and charming!'

'I didn't know her so well then. She came up to me and said, "Oh, Mr Ottley, will you think it rude of me if I suggest that you don't ask dear Elsa out to lunch any more? She said it's so awkward always refusing, but she's not allowed to go out like that without her mother. In fact, though her father is German by birth, she's been brought up quite in the French style. And though, of course, we know you meant no harm, she's positively shocked. You really mustn't flirt with her, Mr Ottley. She doesn't like it. In fact, she asked me to speak to you about it." There was a nice position for me, Edith! Isn't Miss Flummerfelt a treacherous little beast?'

'I thought you said she was so enormously tall. A regal-looking creature was what you called her the first time you met her. Anyhow, you must have been trying to flirt with her, Bruce. I think it rather serves you right. Well, what happened?'

'I said that I was very much astonished at Miss Flummerfelt's misunderstanding me so completely. I even said that some girls have a way of taking everything as if it was meant – in that sort of way, and that I had only asked her to lunch to meet my wife. But, of course, I promised not to do it again. And now it will be rather awful at the rehearsals, because Mrs Mitchell, of course, told her back, and Miss Flummerfelt and I don't speak.'

'Well, after all, it doesn't matter so very much. You only have to announce her. It's with the woman who plays Lady Jenkins you have your longer scene, isn't it? What is she like?'

'Mrs Abbot, do you mean? Oh, I don't think much of her. She's acted before and thinks herself quite as good as a professional, and frightfully smart. She's the most absurd snob you ever saw. She had the cheek to criticise me and say that I don't move about the room naturally, like a real footman. I told her, rather ironically, that I was afraid I'd never been one. So she answered, "Still, you might have seen one." Oh, I have a good deal to go through, one way and another!'

'You'll be glad when it's over, won't you?'

'Very glad. The strain's telling on my health. But I've been better on the whole, I think, don't you?'

'Yes, indeed. You know you have to be,' Edith said.

'Of course – I know. Try not to make me late again tomorrow.'

The solution

A S Sir Charles was walking back from the Reeves' house, he met Anne Yeo in Piccadilly. She had just taken the telegram from Eugenia. He greeted her warmly and asked her to walk a little way with him, to which she agreed, silently giving him credit for so heroically concealing his consciousness of her odd appearance. She herself was well aware that in her mackintosh, driving-gloves, and eternal golf-cap she presented a sufficiently singular effect, and that there were not many people in London at three o'clock on a sunny afternoon who would care to be found dead with her.

'I've just seen Hyacinth,' he said.

'Then you know about the trouble?'

'What trouble?'

'As if she could help telling you! However, it's going to be all right.'

'Do you think so?'

'I'm certain.'

'I never thought him good enough for her,' Sir Charles said.

'Who is?' she asked.

'Has he really been – philandering?'

'Probably. Don't all men?'

'You're as great a cynic as ever, I see,' he laughingly said.

'And you're as noble as ever. But I won't tax your chivalry too far. Good-bye,' and she abruptly left him.

She was on her way to Cook's. She had suddenly decided to emigrate.

Sir Charles wondered why Anne was so sure, but her words had comforted him. He believed her. He not only thought that she must be right, but he instinctively felt certain that she had taken some steps in the matter which would result in success. Some people liked Anne, many detested her, but she inspired in both friends and enemies a species of trust.

At half-past seven that evening Cecil turned the key in the door and went into the house. It was the first time he had ever come home with a feeling of uneasiness and dread; a sensation at once of fear and of boredom. Until now he had always known that he would receive a delighted welcome, all sweetness and affection. He had always had the delicious incense of worshipping admiration swung before him in the perfumed atmosphere of love and peace. Had he held all this too cheaply? Had he accepted the devotion a little pontifically and condescendingly? Had he been behaving like a pompous ass? He had really enjoyed his wife's homage the more because he had liked to think that he still yearned for the impossible, that he had been deprived by Fate of his ideal, that absence and distance had only raised higher in his thoughts the one romantic passion of his life. What a fool he had been! All he felt at this moment about Eugenia was impatient annoyance. There is a great deal of the schoolboy in an Englishman of thirty. Cecil just now regarded her simply as the person who had got him into a row. Why had she taken him for that imprudent drive?

As he went into the little boudoir it happened that Hyacinth was turning her back to him. It was usually a part of their ritual that she came to meet him. So this seemed to him an evil omen.

She stood looking out of the window, very tall, very slender, her brown hair piled in its dense mass on her small head. When she turned round he saw she held a telegram in her hand.

'What is the meaning of this?' she said, as she held it out to him.

He took it from her and sat down to read it, feeling as he did so unpleasantly heavy, stupid, and stolid in contrast to the flash of her blue eyes and the pale tragedy in her face. It was the first time he had ever felt her inferior. As a rule the person found out in a betrayal of love holds, all the same, the superior position of the two. It is the betrayed one who is humiliated.

'What does it mean?' he said. 'Why it means that they have to put us off. They are evidently going away. What it means is fairly obvious.'

'Ah, *why* have they put us off? You have been to see her! You must have arranged this. Yes, you have given me away to her, Cecil; you have let her know I was jealous! It is worse than anything else! I shall never forgive you for this.'

He gave her back the telegram with an air of dazed resignation.

'My dear girl, I give you my solemn word of honour that I know nothing whatever about it.'

'Really? Well, it is very strange. It is most extraordinary! She says she is writing. I suppose we shall hear.'

'Are we going to have dinner?'

'You agree to what I suggested this morning, Cecil?'

'No, I don't.'

'Very well, then; I shan't dine with you.'

'Oh, confound it! I don't want to go out again.'

'Pray don't. I shall dine in my room,' and she walked to the door. As she left the room she turned round and said –

'Oh, to think how that creature must be enjoying it!' and went upstairs.

'If she isn't enjoying it any more than I am, she isn't having much of a time,' said Cecil aloud to himself. He then dined in solemn silence, Hyacinth (with a headache) being served in her own room.

When dinner was over he was glancing through the paper, wondering how he should spend the evening, when a note arrived by a messenger. He saw it was for Hyacinth, and in Eugenia's handwriting.

A few minutes later she came down, holding it in her hand.

'Cecil, she has written to me. She says they're going for a long yachting cruise, that they won't be back in their house for a year.'

'Well, have you any objection?'

'Have you?' she asked, looking at him narrowly.

'No, I'm only too glad!'

'Did you ask her to do this?'

'Don't be idiotic. How could I ask her? I've neither seen nor communicated with her.'

'Then how do you account for it, Cecil?'

'I don't account for it. Why should I? It isn't the first time Uncle Ted's gone yachting. Though he hasn't done it for some years. He was always saying he wanted to go to Crete, Samos, and the Ionian Islands. He used to talk a good deal about wanting to see the Leucadian Rock.'

'What's that?' She spoke suspiciously.

CHAPTER THIRTY-NINE

'A place that some woman threw herself into the sea from.'

'Lately, do you mean?'

'Oh, no – some time ago. Anyhow, he wanted to see it. I'm sure *I* don't know why. But that was his idea.'

'Well, she *says* they're going to Greece, so perhaps you're right. And are you really, really not sorry that she's going?'

'Not at all, if I'm going to have a little peace now.'

'Oh, Cecil,' she implored, 'have I been unfair to you?'

'Horribly unfair.'

'I'm very, very sorry. I see I was wrong. Oh, how could I be so horrid?'

'You *were* down on me! Why, you wanted to go away! You did make me pretty miserable.'

'Oh, poor boy! Then you don't care a bit for that woman, really?'

'Do you mean Eugenia? Not a straw!'

'And, oh, Cecil, if I'm *never* so horrid and bad-tempered again, will you forgive me?'

'Well, I'll try,' said Cecil.

The Bloomsbury Group: a new library of books from
the early twentieth-century

ALSO AVAILABLE IN THE SERIES

RACHEL FERGUSON
THE BRONTËS WENT TO WOOLWORTHS

As growing up in pre-war London looms large in the lives of the Carne sisters, Deirdre, Katrine and young Sheil still cannot resist making up stories as they have done since childhood; from their talking nursery toys to their fulsomely-imagined friendship with real high-court Judge Toddington. But when Deirdre meets the judge's real-life wife at a charity bazaar the sisters are forced to confront the subject of their imaginings. Will the sisters cast off the fantasies of childhood forever? Will Toddy and his wife, Lady Mildred, accept these charmingly eccentric girls? And when fancy and reality collide, who can tell whether Judge Toddington truly wears lavender silk pyjamas or whether the Brontës did indeed go to Woolworths?

*

'Marvellously successful'
A.S BYATT

'The family at its most eccentric and bohemian – a pure concoction of wonderful invention. What an extraordinary meeting I have just had with the Carnes'
DOVEGREYREADER.TYPEPAD.COM

*

ISBN: 978 1 4088 0293 9 · PAPERBACK · £7.99

BLOOMSBURY

JOYCE DENNYS

HENRIETTA'S WAR

NEWS FROM THE HOME FRONT 1939–1942

Spirited Henrietta wishes she was the kind of doctor's wife who knew exactly how to deal with the daily upheavals of war. But then, everyone in her close-knit Devonshire village seems to find different ways to cope: there's the indomitable Lady B, who writes to Hitler every night to tell him precisely what she thinks of him; flighty Faith who is utterly preoccupied with flashing her shapely legs; and then there's Charles, Henrietta's hard-working husband who manages to sleep through a bomb landing in the neighbour's garden.

With life turned upside down under the shadow of war, Henrietta chronicles the dramas, squabbles and loyal friendships of a sparkling community of determined troupers.

✳

'Wonderfully evocative of English middle-class life at the time … never fails to cheer me up'
SUSAN HILL, GOOD HOUSEKEEPING

'Warm and funny, but candid and telling too. A real delight!'
CORNFLOWER.TYPEPAD.COM

✳

ISBN: 978 1 4088 0281 6 · PAPERBACK · £7.99

BLOOMSBURY

FRANK BAKER

MISS HARGREAVES

When, on the spur of a moment, Norman Huntley and his friend Henry invent an eighty-three year-old woman called Miss Hargreaves, they are inspired to post a letter to their new fictional friend. It is only meant to be a silly, harmless game – until she arrives on their doorstep, complete with her cockatoo, her harp and – last but not least – her bath. She is, to Norman's utter disbelief, exactly as he had imagined her: eccentric and endlessly astounding. He hadn't imagined, however, how much havoc an imaginary octogenarian could wreak in his sleepy Buckinghamshire home town, Cornford.

Norman has some explaining to do, but how will he begin to explain to his friends, family and girlfriend where Miss Hargreaves came from when he hasn't the faintest clue himself?

✳

'A fantasy of the most hilarious description – the kind of novel, I fancy, that is badly wanted at the moment, and its central idea is one which has rarely, if, indeed, ever, been used before'
SUNDAY TIMES

'Having met Miss Hargreaves, you won't want to be long out of her company – Frank Baker's novel is witty, joyful, and moving but above all an extraordinary work of the imagination'

STUCK-IN-A-BOOK.BLOGSPOT

✳

ISBN: 978 1 4088 0282 · PAPERBACK · £7.99

BLOOMSBURY

D.E. STEVENSON
MRS TIM

Vivacious, young Hester Christie tries to run her home like clockwork, as would befit the wife of British Army officer, Tim Christie. Left alone for months at a time whilst her husband is with his regiment, Mrs Tim resolves to keep a diary of events large and small in her family life.

When a move to a new regiment in Scotland uproots the Christie family, Mrs Tim is hurled into a whole new drama of dilemmas; from settling in with a new set whilst her husband is away, to disentangling a dear friend from an unsuitable match. And who should stride into Mrs Tim's life one day but the dashing Major Morley, hell-bent on pursuit of our charming heroine. Hester soon finds herself facing unexpected crossroads...

✻

'The writer's unflagging humour, her shrewd, worldly wisdom, and her extremely realistic pictures of garrison life make it all good reading'
TIMES LITERARY SUPPLEMENT

'Delightful domestic comedy'
FRISBEEWIND.BLOGSPOT.COM

✻

ISBN: 978 1 4088 0346 2 · PAPERBACK · £7.99
(PUBLISHED NOVEMBER 2009)

B L O O M S B U R Y

WOLF MANKOWITZ
A KID FOR TWO FARTHINGS

Six year-old Joe knows a unicorn when he sees one. His neighbour Mr Kandinsky has told him all about them, and there isn't anything in the world that this wise tailor doesn't know. So when Joe sees a little white goat in a Whitechapel market he has to have him. He knows it's just a matter of time before the tiny bump on the unicorn's head becomes the magic horn to grant his every wish.

For in the embattled working-class community of 1950s East End London, there are plenty of people in need of good fortune. The only thing Mr Kandinsky wants is a steam press for his shop; his assistant Shmule, a wrestler, just needs to buy a ring for his girl; and all Joe and his mother wish for, more than anything, is to join his father in Africa. But maybe, just maybe, Joe's unicorn can sprinkle enough luck on all his friends for their humble dreams to come true.

✳

'Wolf Mankowitz possessed the now largely vanished gift of being able to write about romance and sentiment without being ever sentimental'
DENNIS NORDEN

'A small miracle. He writes of the teeming streets round the Whitechapel Road with such glowing warmth and love that they come triumphantly alive. Wolf Mankowitz, you are not a star. You are a planet'
DAILY EXPRESS

✳

ISBN: 978 1 4088 0294 6 · PAPERBACK · £7.99
(PUBLISHED NOVEMBER 2009)

ORDER YOUR COPY: BY PHONE +44 (0) 1256 302 699; BY EMAIL: DIRECT@MACMILLAN.CO.UK
DELIVERY IS USUALLY 3–5 WORKING DAYS. FREE POSTAGE AND PACKAGING FOR ORDERS OVER £20.

ONLINE: WWW.BLOOMSBURY.COM/BOOKSHOP
PRICES AND AVAILABILITY SUBJECT TO CHANGE WITHOUT NOTICE.

WWW.BLOOMSBURY.COM/THEBLOOMSBURYGROUP

B L O O M S B U R Y

The History of Bloomsbury Publishing

Bloomsbury Publishing was founded in 1986 to publish books of excellence and originality. Its authors include Margaret Atwood, John Berger, William Boyd, David Guterson, Khaled Hosseini, John Irving, Anne Michaels, Michael Ondaatje, J.K. Rowling, Donna Tartt and Barbara Trapido. Its logo is Diana, the Roman Goddess of Hunting.

In 1994 Bloomsbury floated on the London Stock Exchange and added both a paperback and a children's list. Bloomsbury is based in Soho Square in London and expanded to New York in 1998 and Berlin in 2003. In 2000 Bloomsbury acquired A&C Black and now publishes *Who's Who, Whitaker's Almanack, Wisden Cricketers' Almanack* and the *Writers' & Artists' Yearbook*. Many books, bestsellers and literary awards later, Bloomsbury is one of the world's leading independent publishing houses.

Launched in 2009, The Bloomsbury Group continues the company's tradition of publishing books with perennial, word-of-mouth appeal. This series celebrates lost classics written by both men and women from the early twentieth century, books recommended by readers for readers. Literary bloggers, authors, friends and colleagues have shared their suggestions of cherished books worthy of revival. To send in your recommendation, please write to:

The Bloomsbury Group
Bloomsbury Publishing Plc
36 Soho Square
London
W1D 3QY
Or e-mail: thebloomsburygroup@bloomsbury.com

For more information on all titles in The Bloomsbury Group series and to submit your recommendations online please visit www.bloomsbury.com/thebloomsburygroup

For more information on all Bloomsbury authors and for all the latest news please visit www.bloomsbury.com